# Bones Buried in the Dirt

# BONES BURIED IN THE DIRT

First Edition: January 1st, 2013
All Rights Reserved.
Printed in the United States of America.

Editor: Joseph Michael Owens
Cover Photographer: Timm Burgess

Publishing Editor: Diane Smith

Copyright ©2013 David S. Atkinson

ISBN: 978-0-9835530-3-8


Library of Congress Control Number: 2012947799

American Literature:

1   21ˢᵗ Century
2   Prose Fiction
3   Coming of Age
4   Individual Authors, 2002 – David S. Atkinson

River Otter Press
PO Box 211664
St. Paul, Minnesota 55121

# Bones Buried in the Dirt

*by David S. Atkinson*

RIVER OTTER PRESS | *St. Paul, Minnesota*

For my family and the friends of my early life. You were always better than the flawed characters herein, much better than I usually deserved.

## Publisher's Note

The stories written by David S. Atkinson in this debut collection, according to Mr. Atkinson, are a work of fiction and do not represent anyone he knows. Certain decisions were recommended by the author regarding grammar and tautology to maintain the integrity of the characterizations.

# CONTENTS

# FORWARD

Karen Gettert Shoemaker

I don't know what it's like where you live, but in my
hometown when we get together with old friends the only
topic that comes up more often than who died or who got
divorced is a topic that always ends with the question,
"Good God, how did any of us survive growing up?"

David Atkinson apparently grew up in a town a lot like
mine. His stories take a close look at what exactly adults mean
when they ask that question. Atkinson's narrator in this series of
linked stories is Calvin without the protection of Hobbes. A
child's vulnerabilities are steeped into every scene in such a way
that even as you laugh at (or with) the naiveté of the protagonist
you fear for him—will he make it out alive?

For the most part, the adults in these stories offer little
guidance for how to negotiate the world. More often than not,
they add to the horror of childhood by offering life's lessons in a
confusing array of responses. In "Book Bag" the father tells the
protagonist "never hit a girl!" even as he is hitting him and
screaming in his face. In "Keep Away" he conspires with his son
against one of the weaker neighbor boys by lying and threatening
the neighbor. This story offers one of my favorite scenes in the
collection: Peter running full out toward the safety of his best
friend's front door while being chased by another neighbor boy
who is sniffling and crying behind him. In the end we know it is
Peter running from himself—the boy he does not want to be—
unwanted and alone. But safety, which we see again and again in
this collection, is as illusive as it is elusive.

Atkinson does not flinch, even as he tells the stories
that make you wince to read. His ability to offer the reader what
feels like the real experience of childhood rather than the
recalled experience, results in a collection of stories so unfiltered
by nostalgia and unmitigated by the safety of time and distance
that they are, each and every one, chillingly funny. Sometimes as
you read you don't know if you should laugh or cry. When you
put down this book you might find yourself wanting to hug a

child... or, more likely, grab one by the scruff of the neck and say, "Buck up, Buddy! It gets worse."

I've never understood people who
remember childhood as an idyllic time.

~Bill Watterson, *The Calvin and Hobbes Tenth Anniversary Book*

# Balloon

I wasn't bad, they were. They started it. They shouldn't have gave me the balloon.

At first, I liked my balloon. It was all purple and soft. I liked tossing and catching it. I was even quiet tossing it in the yard. My dad was napping and I wasn't supposed to wake him.

The girl next door to Steven was moving. Her family lived in the grey house on the corner. That's why they gave me the balloon. It was already blown up when they gave it to me.

I liked my balloon, but then I saw my sister's balloon. They'd given her one of those big, banana-shaped ones. It was all long and white with all different color streaks up and down it. Her balloon was all thin and stretchy and smooth. She ran all around our yard with it. The balloon streamed behind her like a pretty ribbon.

I didn't like my balloon anymore.

It wasn't pretty like my sister's. It wasn't fancy. Mine was just ordinary. It was an ugly purple and wasn't smooth or stretchy. Mine wouldn't stream behind me if I ran around our yard. It just sank to the ground like a lump when I tried to throw it up in the air. I used to like doing that, but I didn't anymore.

My balloon made me mad. I hated my balloon.

It wasn't fair. She wasn't supposed to get something I didn't get. It was like cherries in cans of fruit cocktail. Mom always made sure we each got the same number of cherries when she gave us fruit cocktail, to be fair. Neither of us got more than the other. If there were extras, Mom ate them.

One time my sister got the fruit cocktail for us. She gave herself more cherries than me. I told her she couldn't do that and she told me it didn't matter and that I should be quiet. I told Dad. She got spanked for not sharing the cherries and she didn't try telling me it didn't matter again.

The balloons were just like cherries.

I went and told them, just like the cherries. I took my balloon back and told the little girl's mom that I didn't want my balloon anymore. I wanted one like they'd given my sister. I gave her mine back.

The girl's mom got mad. She told me they didn't have any more. She took mine.

"I thought since you were going to be in kindergarten soon, Peter," she snapped, "that you were old enough to handle a gift. Apparently I was mistaken."

Then she went back in her house and slammed the screen door. She took my balloon.

She took my balloon and acted like *I'd* done something bad. She was mean. Kids sometimes don't know better but adults have to act good. I should've told my dad so he would've told her how bad she was.

Then I got sad. She had my balloon. I didn't have any balloon anymore. I didn't want to have no balloon. I cried.

It was good they were moving. They weren't nice. I hated them. I wanted them to go away. Go away and not come back.

My sister let her balloon float to the ground while she was running around and twirling it in the air. It popped. It popped when it touched the grass, the real thick kind of grass that's rough and pointy at the end, not the soft brown grass in most people's yards. It made her cry. She only had the balloon a couple hours. She only got to have it a couple hours and it made her cry.

My dad got mad because my sister wouldn't stop crying. He heard her all the way inside the house. He heard her and came outside to make her stop crying. She wouldn't stop because she was sad her balloon popped and he got mad because she wouldn't stop. He gave her something to cry about.

I wished they'd never lived there at all. All they did was make little kids cry.

## Wooden Nickel Payback

I ran to my friend Steven's house. His was the white stucco one across the street. I jumped up onto Steven's top porch step, leaping over the other ones. Really high and really fast. That was because of my TRON shirt under my coat. The hand-me-down one from my cousin. It was good that I wore it. I opened the porch door and walked in.

My sister came over earlier to play with Steven's sister, but I had to empty the dishwasher before I could. We could all play hide and seek again. Last time I kept losing and it made me mad. This time it'd be different, though. I'd be *it* all the time. Steven said that was good practice for when we grew up to be bounty hunters. I'd catch them all. Because of my shirt.

Steven opened the door when I knocked. "What?" He was wearing one of his dad's old Marine hats. The green one that looked like a cowboy hat with one side folded up. His cheeks were all red, like he'd been running.

"I came over to play."

"So?" He tilted his chin up so the hat slipped back on his head. It almost fell off, but it had a rope attached to it that caught on his chin. His hair underneath looked all sticky and sweaty. "I don't want to play with you."

"Huh?" My sister was already inside playing with his sister. I heard them laughing somewhere inside. Probably down in the basement. If he let me in we could play hide and seek again.

Steven leaned out, grabbing the brass knob and the oak doorframe to hold himself up. He swung back and forward like that. "We're playing and you can't. Go home." His face was screwed up, all nasty like. I hadn't done anything. He didn't have anything to be mad about.

"But…why?"

"Because I don't want to," he snorted, pulling himself up in the air and kicking his feet at me like he was on a swing. He had on his dad's jungle boots which barely stayed on his feet. "We're having fun and you can't join. Go play by yourself."

"You can't all just play and make me go," I told him. "That isn't fair."

"Yes I can," he snapped. "It's my house." His teeth chattered as he talked. It made me think of the monkeys at the zoo.

"I'll tell." My eyes blurred like I was going to cry. I tried to stop so he wouldn't see.

"I don't care. *Tell.*" He pinched up his face, pretending it was me saying it but all high and whiny. "Then my dad will say you can't come in if I don't want you to."

"Come on," I pleaded.

Steven slammed the door. The lace curtain over the door's little windows shook.

I didn't go anywhere.

Their porch was walled with big storm windows. It was kind of inside, but outside. There was a bunch of toys and kitchen stuff on the porch along with some yard things that belonged on a porch. I started messing around. Maybe Steven would think I'd break something and let me inside to stop me. I found his Speak and Read under a dusty white metal wire chair, but it didn't have any batteries. His Styrofoam plane was sticking out of some dirt in an empty clay planter, but Steven had already broken that so it wasn't any better.

"Peter?"

I turned around, but it wasn't Steven. It was Steven's mom. She was big and fat and old with a puff of curly brown hair. She always seemed real nice, though. She made cookies and stuff. She smiled.

"They're all inside and won't let me play," I told her real quick. "Steven's just being mean. Can I come in, too?" I gasped out in one breath.

She stared, eyes wide. "Well," she finally said, shifting around like she was nervous about something. "I don't think we should make them play with you if they don't want to."

"But," I stammered, "he's just being mean."

"I know, dear," she responded. "Still, for today, why don't you just go play at your house? They'll probably play with you tomorrow." She stood there in the doorway and didn't say anything else. I left slowly and she watched me until I closed the porch door behind me.

I slumped back over to my house. I didn't even look up when I crossed the street, but no cars were in the street or on the block anyway. Steven and them were probably doing something fun like playing freeze tag. I bet they all laughed because I got sent home. I sat in the living room on our puffy blue couch with the circles on it and hated them.

I wanted to get Steven back. He needed to be sorry. I wished I had something fun so he'd want to come over, and then I wouldn't let him in. I couldn't think of anything, though. We had cable, but our TV was little. Not like Steven's big old console set. He said regular TV was better than cable, anyway. My dad's Atari was on the floor, but I wasn't supposed to hook it up. I didn't have anything really cool, not like Steven's headchopper.

He'd showed it to me one time. He just put peoples' heads inside and they'd get cut off. Disappeared, so he couldn't get in trouble because no one would find anything. He said it was like a trapdoor so it never needed sharpening. It was by the side door to the basement, hidden back by the walk between Steven's house and his neighbor's. That's why his parents didn't know. They never looked back there. He'd built it in secret while they were doing other stuff.

I didn't have anything like that.

I looked out the windows at Steven's house. That was it. I'd show him. I took a butter knife from the kitchen drawer. One of the thick old heavy ones with the weird swirls on it. It'd work good. It was strong and wouldn't break.

The kitchen drawer banged when I shut it. One of the plastic wheels inside had popped off the rail. I listened, but it was quiet. My mom was at work and my dad was up in his room with the door closed again. Probably reading magazines. I sometimes heard pages flip when I walked by up there. Probably *National Geographic.* Those were boring, but they were the only magazines we had. I hid the butter knife in my coat and snuck out the front door.

No one saw me when I walked over because I didn't knock again. I walked right over to the side of the house instead. Steven's dad had been raking leaves, but he'd just left them in a messy pile by some black trash bags. He wasn't outside anymore. I walked in the cyclone fence gate to the walkway between the houses. The one that led past the basement door to Steven's backyard. No one could see the headchopper back there so no one would see me.

When I got there, though, I didn't know what to do. I could see the headchopper all right, but there wasn't anything to break. It looked just like a block of wood in the wall with the stucco busted all around it. It didn't even budge when I pushed. There weren't any buttons or anything. It just wouldn't open. There must have been some secret Steven hadn't told me. I guessed all the stuff to break was on the inside, but there was no way to get at it. I had to figure it out. Sooner or later someone would look out a window or come looking.

If I couldn't break it, I'd at least do something. I took the butter knife and stuck it over and over. It chewed up the wood pretty good. Carved out little chips and made hollow thucking noises.

After I messed it up as much as I could, I hid the knife back in my coat and ran home. I made sure I closed the gate so no one knew I'd been there. Steven's dad hadn't come back. The leaf pile was the same other than moving around a little in the wind. I even put the butter knife back in the kitchen. Then no one could find out. It was perfect.

Except it wasn't. My dad burst in the kitchen when I was sitting on one of the wooden stools at the linoleum counter, eating my lunch. Not the counter between the sink and stove with the cabinets, the one that stuck out from the wall in part of a circle with nothing underneath it. Lunch was carrot sticks and a baloney sandwich with mustard, not mayonnaise. He came in so fast I almost choked.

"What the hell were you doing?" He yelled. His neck was all knotted up like when he was screaming at cars in traffic. "Answer me!"

"What?" I croaked, starting to cry. I couldn't help it.

"At Steven's! What were you doing at Steven's?"

"Nothing! Nancy and Lauren and Steven were all playing but wouldn't let me. They made me go home."

He slammed his hand down on the counter and a couple of my carrot sticks jumped off my plate. He shook his finger in my face, his fist balled up tight. I thought he was going to hit me. "Steven's dad called and said you hacked up the side of his house!"

I was bawling. He yelled right next to my face. His spit hit me. He'd shaved off his beard and mustache, but there were still a few short little brown hairs on his neck. Since he just stayed at home he didn't have to shave every day. I guess he wasn't good at it anymore. His chin looked all small and scraped red, greasy. I couldn't answer.

"You vandalized their house! I raised you better than that!"

"No! It was just the headchopper!"

My dad snapped back. Then the mad drained all out of him, like that time downtown when he found out that homeless guy he'd yelled at for asking for money got a fake leg in the war. "The what?" It was his inside voice.

"I had to break it," I lied and went on, not sure if I should cry or not. Maybe he thought it was good because Steven shouldn't have had it. "Steven could've hurt somebody."

"A headchopper?" My dad blinked, like he couldn't believe Steven had one. He must've told that I broke it, but not what it was. Now they'd know. He'd probably get grounded. "A headchopper!" He seemed relieved. Almost happy. "That's what you thought it was?"

He wasn't yelling, but something felt weird. He wasn't laughing in a good way. "Steven built it secret so nobody would know."

"Why did you believe that?" He leaned in close again over the kitchen counter. He smiled, but that was wrong, too.

"Steven said so." I was starting to cry again. It wasn't a headchopper. Steven lied. My dad asked the question like that because he knew it wasn't true. My eyes were getting blurry. He wasn't yelling or hitting, but I was still crying. He just kept staring at me. It was worse than him yelling or hitting. I wished he'd just hit me. Even with his heavy leather belt.

"Do you know what you hacked up?"

"No," I sniffed. My nose was running. There was snot in my mouth.

"Steven's dad fixed a hole with a piece of plywood. That's what you chopped up, your headchopper. He hadn't covered it in stucco and painted it yet."

"I'm sorry," I wailed. "I didn't mean to!"

"You didn't hurt anything," my dad said, kind of calm by then. He rubbed his forehead. "All you did was mess up the plywood. Glen can still just slather some stucco on and paint it."

I wiped my nose on my arm. I didn't show Steven anything. I hadn't taken anything away from him. Steven and his sister and my sister were probably all over there laughing. They knew because they knew about the hole. I'd been dumb and they all knew it.

But...that still meant that Steven never had anything as neat as a headchopper. Even if I was dumb enough to believe him, he was the one who pretended to seem special. If he actually had anything else that cool, he wouldn't have made stuff up. He wasn't so great. I smiled.

"The next time Steven tells you something," my dad said, leaning in again, scowling because I wasn't paying enough attention, "you remember that he's a damn liar."

# The War

I zipped up my coat. It was dumb. It wasn't even that cold out that day, but my mom made me wear it anyway. She said I couldn't go out to play without it. It was too bulky to be able to run around in good 'cause it was all thick and stiff and blue. It wasn't even one I got to pick out. My grandma got it for my birthday when I turned six. At least I hadn't had to wear my mittens too.

I saw Jeff over with Steven as I came out of my porch. It looked like they were playing football out in the street. Jeff was standing over Steven like he was blocking and Steven was all crouched down hiding a ball like he was trying to keep it away from Jeff. It didn't look so hard. All Steven had to do was run around. Jeff was tall, but he was skinny. That was no good for playing football. Steven could have run either way and won.

I started to hurry. I thought maybe Jeff and PJ had come over to play. They lived a couple blocks over so they only came to play once in a while. It was fun when they did. We got to do different stuff because it wasn't just me and Steven or me and Nicky. I didn't see PJ, though. Nicky was there, but he wasn't over by Jeff and Steven. He was standing off all by himself, just looking.

"Cut it out," Steven yelled at Jeff. "It's mine!"

Jeff pushed Steven and knocked him down. Nicky just looked at them.

I grabbed a log from the pile next to my porch. It was from that big branch that fell in the backyard. I hadn't been able to play back there for a week because the branch was all over and my dad had said I'd get hurt. Then he chopped it up and said we were really going to have fires in the fireplace that year. It all just sat there, though, next to the porch.

I ran at them and held the log above my head with both hands. I yelled really loud. I went right for Jeff.

He looked up at me suddenly when he heard me yell. I didn't think he even knew I had come outside. He saw I had quick enough, though. He turned and started running fast down the block before I got to him. He was all the way to the alley and disappeared behind Nicky's house before I stopped running.

I dropped the log. My dad would have gotten mad if he saw me. I wasn't supposed to play with sticks. Logs were probably sticks.

"Run, you chicken," Steven shouted after Jeff. He got up from where Jeff knocked him down. Nicky walked over.

"What happened?" I asked.

Steven clutched a football. "He tried to say this was his. It's mine. He was just trying to take it."

I frowned. I liked PJ and Jeff. They had just come walking up one day while we were playing freeze tag and asked if they could play too. They looked kind of funny together. PJ was really short and had a buzz cut. Jeff was really tall and had dark brown hair. We had thought they were really cool, even if they did look funny together. They even said they had a junkyard at their house.

But they weren't cool.

I couldn't see why Jeff would have done something like that. We were their friends and Jeff had tried to take Steven's stuff. Friends didn't do that. Friends shared. Steven hadn't done anything to him.

"He said it was his." Nicky wiped his nose on his sleeve and sniffed.

"He lied! He just said that so he could take it," Steven yelled at Nicky. "Why're you even here? I'm not playing with you! You're always hanging around and nobody likes you. Go home!"

Nicky didn't say anything back.

Steven rolled the football around in his hands. "I told him if it was his then where did he leave it. He said he left it up on the hill by the graveyard but I found it over on the sidewalk by Nicky's all the way across the alley. I found it fair and square and he wanted to steal it by lying and saying he just left it somewhere and was hoping he'd guess right and I'd believe him."

"You didn't fall for it, though."

"Nope," he smiled. "That's why I made him tell me where he left it first. He asked me where I found it but I wasn't going to tell him until he told me. He was going to say he left it where I said I found it. I'm not stupid."

Nicky looked over at his yard. "Maybe it rolled down the hill."

"Don't be a dummy!" Steven threw the football at Nicky.

Nicky flinched, but it hit him anyway. He shrunk away a little. Then he bent down to grab the football and handed it back to Steven. Steven caught it and smacked it a couple of times.

"He's a jerk," I said and looked where Jeff ran off. "He should get his own toys. He shouldn't lie and try to take yours."

"Yeah." Steven smacked the ball again, like he was getting ready to throw it. "Well, they're in for it now."

"In for what?" I looked at him.

"We're at war." Steven grinned. He looked mean like that. I looked at Nicky. "Their block and our block—it's us against them." He threw the football in the air and caught it.

*****

Nicky ran. I ran after him.

"It's over here," Nicky said. "I found it this morning but I bet it's still there."

"Why'd she throw it out?"

"I dunno. She could get fifty or sixty cents by turning them in but she just threw them away. Maybe she doesn't know you can get money for empties."

We ran up by the trashcans and there was a white cardboard box sitting next to the cans. It wasn't big, like a couple things of soda stuck together. It had *BEER* written in big black letters on the side.

"See," Nicky said, pulling open the box. The top lifted open like somebody had cut all the way around and just left one side hanging on. Like a trapdoor. Inside was a bunch of crisscrossing cardboard pieces. Like Honeycomb cereal. A bunch of little boxes inside the big box. There was a brown glass bottle in each of the little boxes.

"We can throw them," I suggested. "We'll need weapons for the war."

"Yeah. Maybe Steven will even let me throw one since I found them for you guys. PJ and Jeff got the junkyard so we need something, too."

"The junkyard's nothing special," I shrugged. I'd seen it. I snuck over one time even though I wasn't supposed to leave the block. I followed them past the block over and cut through a space behind a garage to their block. The junkyard was just an old garden on the side of PJ's house with nothing growing in it. There was just some pipes and sticks in it. It hadn't been worth getting grounded.

I even had to find my own way home. I had tried to go the long way around because they said the guy with the garage got mad if you walked through there more than once. The street hadn't looked right, though, and I wasn't able to find my way back. I just ran through the space behind the garage so the guy wasn't able to catch me.

"There's no beer in them, is there? We'll get in trouble if we have beer."

"No." Nicky looked around. "Nobody's looking anyway. No one will know if we take them."

I grabbed the box and we both ran off toward the alley. We stopped just around the corner from his house and looked to see if anybody was following us. The block was quiet.

"We got to figure out what to do with them."

"My mom might let me keep them in the garage," Nicky offered.

I shook my head. "That won't work. PJ and Jeff would get us before we got to the bottles. We got to have them ready to throw."

I looked around. I though maybe we could have kept them on the side of Nicky's house. They would have been right there. Then I remembered Nicky's dad kept their trash there. He would have just thrown them out. I shifted the box. It was getting heavy, even though the bottles were all empty.

"I got it! Let's hide them in the hole in that tree up there." I pointed up at the hill to the graveyard. "PJ and Jeff won't find them and we can run there when they attack. Then we can throw the bottles down so they can't follow."

"Yeah!"

"Now we just got to get them to chase us."

*****

"Quick!" Steven ran up to me.

"Huh?"

"I just saw PJ and Jeff! We can get them! You gotta come!"

Then he turned and ran off toward the alley. I'd been rolling my dump truck on my sidewalk. There'd been snow everywhere for a while but it finally all melted so I hadn't been allowed to play outside for a while. I got up and ran with Steven.

We ran through Nicky's yard. I guessed they were down that way. I saw a broom as we were running and I stopped.

"What're you doing? Hurry up!"

"Getting a weapon," I said. I grabbed at the broom and I started running again. The broom part came away and I was just running with the pole. Good. A broom wasn't as scary as a staff. Then I looked like a ninja.

We went running down the alley and out onto the next block. I ran and didn't think about it because we had to catch them, but I wasn't supposed to be off the block. I started worrying, but I didn't seem to slow down. I was running even faster than Steven. He was falling way behind.

"You're going to get us?" PJ yelled at Nicky. PJ and Jeff had him between them. PJ pushed Nicky at Jeff. Then Jeff pushed him back at PJ. "Come on and get us," PJ said, pushing Nicky back at Jeff again. "I dare you."

"*Aaaaaahh!*" I ran at them, swinging the broomstick above my head and yelling like a ninja. They moved apart as I charged. PJ ran off and even Nicky got out of the way. Jeff just stood there. He did back up a little, though.

I'd been all ready. I was going to run in and just swing at somebody. It didn't really matter who. Just swing. Run in and hit. *Smack!*

I pulled back, though. I almost tripped because I was running up so fast swinging and I had to try to stop so I didn't just run into Jeff. Steven almost ran into me, too.

I held the broomstick like a staff. Steven got on one side of Jeff and Nicky got on the other. Jeff held up his fists like he was going to punch one of us. He looked back and forth at us all real quick, like he was trying to see us all at the same time. PJ ditched him. It was three against one then.

"Hit him!" Steven pointed at Jeff.

I whipped an end of the broomstick at Jeff. I didn't hit him. I just scared him. He flinched. Then I did it again.

"Come on," Steven ordered. "Get him!"

"Yeah," Nicky said. "He can't get away."

Jeff looked to each of them when they talked. He looked back at me when I swung my staff again. I still didn't hit him.

I was going to hit him. I was just getting ready. I had to get ready. I couldn't have just hit him without getting ready. It was hard to swing the broomstick around with my coat all zipped up, too. Especially with the hood on. It was tough to move.

"Do it!"

I went to swing for real that time, but something hard hit my head. It made a pop sound. It felt kind of like a *whap*, though.

Jeff froze and his mouth hung open. Steven and Nicky were looking like that, too. Their eyes were all open wide.
No-body moved; they were waiting on something.

I turned around. PJ was standing there. He must have been the one that snuck up, but nothing was in his hands.

There was stuff all over me. I shook a little and it started falling to the cement, tinkling. Pieces of brown glass.

I looked at the pieces as they fell. I sort of stared. Then I saw PJ running away down the alley toward his block. Jeff was running the other way around. Steven and Nicky still looked at me after PJ and Jeff ran out of sight. I wondered if I had got cut. I put my hand up to check.

"Wow! That was awesome," Steven said when I started feeling my head to see if I was okay. Nicky looked over at him. Steven looked back at him and then at me. "You just got a bottle broke over your head and you didn't get hurt or nothing!"

I was still checking my head. I didn't think I had got hurt. I couldn't decide whether I wanted to cry or not.

"Wasn't that awesome?" Steven asked Nicky after I didn't say anything.

"Yeah," Nicky agreed.

"You must be invincible or something," Steven continued, "or like have a super-strong head. Nobody else could get hit like that and not get hurt. Not me."

"You think so?" I finally asked.

"Yeah! Did you see how they ran off? We won! They won't be back after seeing something like that."

Nicky nodded.

I looked over where PJ ran off and then where Jeff ran off. I didn't see them coming back. I guessed we won.

# Book Bag

"Hey, Peter," Anne said.

Anne and Heather walked up to me. School had just gotten out. Kids were running round everywhere. I was coming down the sidewalk outside my school so my dad could pick me up.

"What do you want?" I said.

They were both in my class. Anne was annoying. She was always messing with me. She even called me one time and pretended she couldn't speak English. I could tell it was her, though. Some prank. Heather usually tagged along with Anne, but she didn't talk much.

"Pick a number," Anne said. She had one of those dumb folding paper things girls were always playing with on her fingers.

"Why should I?"

"Come on," she pushed the paper thing at me. It had points sticking all over the place and there was girly writing on it. Purple and green ink. "I'll tell your future."

My book bag was getting heavy. I wanted to put it down. It was like a grocery bag with handles. It didn't have straps so I couldn't put it on my back. My parents said I should get a backpack, but I wanted this bag because it had Garfield on it. It was light blue. I couldn't put it down because the ground was wet. It rained all day during school. That was why I wore my plastic yellow raincoat. It wasn't raining anymore, but I still had to hold my book bag.

"I got to go. My dad's waiting." My dad didn't like it if I kept him waiting.

"This'll just take a second," Anne insisted. "Pick a number."

Heather stood there. She smiled, but it wasn't funny. She looked like they were up to something.

"Fine. Two"

Anne crinkled the paper thing, folding it different ways. "Okay, now pick a letter. D, f, a, or g."

"G." I rolled my eyes.

Anne was pudgy. Not really fat, but a little. She always wore her hair up in a ponytail. Brown and frizzy. She kind of looked like a bulldog. Heather was prettier. She was skinny and had long black hair. She acted snotty, though.

Anne giggled. "Now pick four girls in our class."

"How long is this going to take?"

She bugged her eyes out at me. "Almost done! Pick four. Doesn't matter who."

"Fine," I sighed. "Stacie, Shawna, Beckie, and LaShelle." I just picked the girls that sat by me so I could go.

"Okay," Anne crinkled the paper some more.

"Well?"

They both giggled.

"When you grow up," Anne said, acting like she was reading off the paper, "you're going to live in a trailer. You'll work as a garbage man and marry LaShelle!"

Both of them started laughing.

"No I won't!" I yelled, but they kept laughing. "That's just a stupid piece of paper. None of that is going to happen."

"Yeah it is," Anne insisted. "You're going to get married to LaShelle!"

LaShelle was a fat black girl who sat right in front of me. Real fat. Not a little pudgy like Anne. She was the fattest kid in the class. Her hair always looked wet and smelled weird. I would never have picked her if I knew what I was picking for.

"Peter likes LaShelle! Peter likes LaShelle!"

"I do not. Stop it!"

She ran off, still shouting it. Heather ran with her. I chased after, yelling at her to quit. They weren't running real fast so it wasn't hard to keep up.

I swung my book bag, but it barely got Anne. They both just laughed more. Then I stopped. They were dumb. Saying stuff didn't make it true. I didn't even like them anyway.

I hurried. My dad got mad if I took too long. I wasn't supposed to play around after school, just get to the car. He said he wasn't going to just sit around all day and wait.

The car was across the street. I made sure to cross at the cross walk so my dad wouldn't get mad at that, too. Then I got in and buckled my seat belt.

My dad stared ahead. He didn't start the car.

"I got an A-plus on my social studies test today," I said, hoping that would make him forget I hadn't come straight there. "It was really hard, too. We had to know all about the pilgrims, but I knew it and I got almost all the questions right. I just missed a couple—"

"What was that?" he yelled. His head snapped toward me. "Want to tell me what that was all about?"

My ears stung. He yelled really loud and the windows were all up.

"Anne wanted to tell my future except not for real. Then I came right over."

I was already crying. I didn't care if anybody at school could see me. It just came out anyway.

"And then you hit her," he screamed in my face. I could even feel his yelling, not just hear it.

"I just swung my bag," I pleaded. "It didn't hurt her or nothing. She laughed at me and said I liked LaShelle Johnson. I told her to stop but she wouldn't."

"I don't care what she did!"

He was yelling though gritted teeth. His whole body was shaking, like he could barely control himself. I tried to shrink away, but there was nowhere to go. Red poured into his face.

"I–"

He slammed his hand down on my leg. Over and over again. I screamed. My leg burned. I was bawling so hard everything was blurry and I couldn't see.

Then he stopped quick. He glared. I didn't dare say anything. My lower lip trembled.

"You *never* hit a girl! I don't care what they do to you. If they make fun of you then you take it like a man. If they hit you, then walk away. Never! *Never* hit a girl."

I could hardly breathe. He was still tensed up and shaking. I thought he might hit me some more.

"Got that?"

I nodded.

"I asked you if you got that! Don't just shake your head. I want you to answer me."

"*Yes*," I wailed.

He turned back forward again and gripped the wheel with both hands. "When we get home, I want you to go right to your room," he told me. "Don't even think about crying to your mom either." Then he started the car and drove off.

## Zoom Rainbow

**"Y**ou got to do it." Steven pointed without looking up at the cement steps at the end of the front walk in the middle of my yard. "You'll go right through the air, like the A-Team."

The block was quiet. It was morning in the summer so we didn't have school, but it was a weekday so nobody else was outside in their yards. Just me and my best friend, Steven, and that jerk, Freddy, who Steven was always hanging out with.

I kicked at my blue big wheel's pedals, rocking back and forth on the sidewalk in front of my house. I looked at the steps. They were so square the edges looked sharp. "I don't know. You'd have to go really fast."

Freddy smirked, wrinkling his face up. "You're just chicken." He swung his handlebars, turning his front wheel. "I could make it."

"No I'm not!" I looked quick at Steven, but he was just sitting on his red and yellow big wheel. His brown hair hadn't been cut in a while so his ears didn't stick out so much like they usually did. "Why don't *you* do it, Freddy?"

Freddy looked off down the block, like he was looking in the street for cars even though there weren't any. "I can't. My mom said she just bought me this and I had to take good care of it. She'll put it away if I scratch it all up."

"Yeah," Steven agreed, "yours is all old anyway. Just peddle as hard as you can."

Steven's was just as old as mine. Not all new like Freddy's. I don't even know why Freddy's parents got him a new green and white one. His last one was fine, barely even scraped up at all yet—just a little on the black plastic wheels.

Steven and Freddy stared at me. Finally, I stood up and dragged my big wheel between my legs up the hill. Steven and

Freddy rolled their big wheels down the sidewalk each way away from the steps. I tried to think how it wasn't very far down. Just a couple steps. I got all the way back up the front walk. By the white metal storm door to my porch. The steps looked far away, but maybe not far enough to get going fast enough. I sat there a while and Steven and Freddy looked sick of waiting.

Suddenly, I peddled. I don't remember starting, but the steps flew at me. The street on the other side of them too. I started thinking about crashing. Tumbling down the stairs or skidding all over the street. Just before I hit the end of the front walk I swerved to the right instead and rolled down the grass hill of my yard. I stopped at the bottom when I got to the sidewalk.

"You didn't do it." Steven complained.

"Chicken," Freddy added. He smiled big and smug. His face always looked like it was nothing but that stupid smile and his dumb yellow hair when he did that.

"No! I was doing it. I skidded on accident."

Steven frowned, like he didn't believe me. He picked up his big wheel. For a second, I thought maybe he'd do it and it'd be easy. Luckily, he turned it over so the front wheel was up in the air. He grabbed a plastic pedal and spun, grinding the end of the stick he grabbed from my yard on the thin spinning front wheel. I did too. Doing that wore the end of the stick to a point, though you had to peel the bark back to get it to grind right— like a spear.

Freddy didn't make a spear like me and Steven. He probably thought he was too cool for spears. He had a stick, though. He just broke it little by little and tore off the bark. Then he tossed the pieces onto the grass. One piece was too small to break again. His face turned red and he tried really hard to break it over his knee. He looked funny, how red his face got with how yellow his hair was. Then he stopped and tossed it into the grass when he saw me looking.

"We need some dog poop," Steven suggested. "Not hard crusty stuff either. Some that's still soft." Steven stopped turning the wheel and blew on the end of the stick, for some reason. "We'll stick the points in it. It's like poison."

"Really?" I looked at Steven. Freddy did, too.

"Sure. The Dixies do it with their knives and stuff. If you get cut with it, even doctors can't do anything."

"Dixies?" Freddy'd run out of stick to break.

"Those girls that live out in the wilderness in Colorado. Out by Cripple Creek. My cousin knows them. They camp out all the time and shoot guns. Nobody stops them because even the sheriffs are afraid of them." He looked up at us. "You've heard about them, right?"

Freddy looked up at a squirrel in one of the trees in my yard. "Sure."

I bet Freddy hadn't. He just couldn't admit someone knew something he didn't. "Me too," I jumped in. I couldn't be the only one that hadn't known, not since Freddy lied.

"They do what they want," he went on. "I'm going to join them. Then I wouldn't have to go to school or anything."

"Peter!" My dad leaned out the front porch door. He was wearing his cutoffs and his old twenty-fifth infantry shirt. "That better not be a stick I see you playing with!"

I dropped it. My dad went back inside. "Maybe I'll do that too."

Steven curled his lip. "You can't. If they see you they'll stick you." He jabbed his spear at me. "Only I can go because they know my cousin."

I wanted to pick up my stick and jab back, but I didn't. "We could go with you," I suggested. I picked at the pizza scratch and sniff sticker on the bottom of my big wheel. I put all my extras on there so I didn't junk up my sticker book with a bunch of copies.

Steven scrunched up his face, and closed one eye, like he was thinking. "I'll take you, but you got to keep up or I'll leave you behind."

"I can keep up," Freddy countered. "I can do it if you guys can."

"We got to plan too," Steven said quietly, looking around. "We got to be ready."

"Plan? Like what?"

"We've got to make a codeword," Steven sighed and rolled his eyes. "If people hear us say 'running away' they'll know what we're talking about."

"How about softball? We could say playing softball." I kept spinning my pedal, even though I didn't have a stick anymore.

Steven shook his head. "That's stupid. We might actually need to talk about softball. Anyway, that's got nothing to do with running away. It's got to be something that means it but doesn't." I looked at him and waited. Freddy didn't say anything, he was probably afraid to look like a dork if it wasn't any good. "I got it! It'll be like camp sign language." He made like his fingers were running. Then he swung his arm. "See? Run and away. It looks like zoom and rainbow."

"Zoom and rainbow?" I didn't say that sounded stupid too, but it did.

"Yeah, Zoom Rainbow." Steven spun his wheel really fast. "Whenever we say that we'll know it means run away but nobody else will."

Freddy sat down on his big wheel. "I'm not going. My mom said I could have a pizza party for my birthday."

I looked at Steven. "You're not going just so you can have a pizza party?" Still, I didn't get to have pizza parties for my birthday. Just a party at the house with cake and ice cream. Steven hadn't had a pizza party either.

"So what?" He jumped up and pushed me. "Don't go to my party then! I don't care!"

I pushed him back. "Scaredy-cat!"

He turned around and grabbed his big wheel. He didn't even push me again. I bet he was too scared to run away. Not like me and Steven. We'd do it. We probably weren't going to, though, since Freddy was too chicken. He'd tell. Steven shouldn't have told him. I smiled.

Steven paused. "Is it going to be at Pefferonis?"

"Probably," Freddy said. His face was nothing but a sneer. "My mom will let me have it wherever I want because it's my birthday."

"We'll just run away after your birthday," Steven said. "Then we can all go." Freddy looked down at his nice new big wheel. I looked down at mine, too.

\*\*\*\*\*

I stood on the straw doormat by our back door over by the downstairs bathroom. Through the kitchen, I tried to hear where everybody was. My dad was still upstairs in bed, sleeping late. My mom and sister were upstairs too. Probably doing something in my sister's room. I swallowed.

I shuffled my feet back and forth. I was supposed to be in the kitchen, eating my breakfast. Captain Crunch with Crunch Berries. One foot kept moving to do that. The other one kept moving to go out the back door. I needed to go outside, but all my feet did were shuffle.

It was quiet. No one was downstairs. They wouldn't notice. Sooner or later someone would come down the stairs, though, and I'd miss my chance. I decided I wanted breakfast. Then I wanted to go outside. Then I wanted breakfast again.

I started thinking I'd need stuff for Zoom Rainbow. I went and grabbed the plastic camouflage bag my mom got at Canfield's. We could carry stuff in it. It was square and it had metal rings in the plastic that the strap went through so it pinched closed when I picked it up. There was some hard thing in the bottom so it held a lot but still sat flat. I put a pair of my Superman pajamas inside.

I turned the brass bolt on the back door and it clicked really loud. I tried not to breath, but it was still quiet. Slowly, I turned the knob. Then I inched the door open when the knob didn't turn anymore. The door was open and I still didn't hear anything so I pushed the latch on the storm door. It creaked just a little as it opened.

All I had to do then was walk outside. Outside was right there. I bit my lip. I never went outside without asking or I'd get grounded. The door was open. It'd be Zoom Rainbow if I went outside. I looked at the kitchen. There was cereal in there. I was supposed to pour myself some and eat it.

Then I saw my feet moving. I stepped outside and slowly pulled the door shut. I hoped it was quiet. I held the screen door so it didn't slam. Quickly, I jumped off the deck. They were all upstairs. They could see me if they looked so I ran around the side of the house and kept running past the front.

Steven said he was going to wait around the corner on Freddy's block. He'd wait just for a while. Me and Freddy could come with him if we showed. It was still pretty early. The grass was still wet and no one was outside yet, even though it was already light out. Steven said that was good. That way we'd be too far to catch by the time anyone knew we were gone.

I stopped running after I got to the corner. I had to turn and go over to Freddy's block, but I didn't ever go off my block. I wasn't allowed.

Well, I'd been over there before. My parents drove that way whenever we went to Hinky Dinky or Target. Burger King too. Just never by myself. I was only allowed to walk around on my block on my own.

When I got to the corner I tried to see down to where Steven was, but it was hard to see that far. The sun was shining really bright too. It made everything on the next block look washed out. I put my hand over my eyes, but it didn't help much. I couldn't tell whether Steven was there or not. I stopped walking. I wasn't going down there if Steven wasn't. I thought maybe I saw him. Maybe.

Then I got an idea. I waved my arms. He'd see me and wave too. That I'd see for sure. Nobody waved back, though. Not that I could tell. It wasn't Zoom Rainbow after all. I had to get home.

I ran back around the corner and back around the house. No one was outside still. I stepped carefully onto the deck and peeked in the back door. The coast was clear so I snuck in and hid the bag in the bathroom. Then I ran to get the cereal.

"What the hell were you doing?" My dad screamed and grabbed my arm. His bushy hair shook when he yelled. It was all matted and sticking up in parts, like he'd just got out of bed and come downstairs. He pulled and spun me around toward the den. I hadn't seen him hiding there. My shoulder hurt.

"I think you're down here eating and then I see you outside? You don't ever go outside without telling us! Do you want somebody to kidnap you? Do you want us to find you dead in a ditch?"

He wrenched me close and started spanking me. I jumped away from the smack each time he hit me, but then he pulled my arm to snap me back again. I cried, but he didn't stop when I started crying. He was so mad it even looked like he was crying. Then he tore at my arm to spin me around. He pulled me that way into the kitchen and threw me at one of the stools. I bounced off the kitchen counter and he pushed me down onto the stool.

"Now sit down. And don't let me see you outside again without telling me first!"

Then I had to eat my breakfast.

*****

That afternoon, Steven was out in his front yard. His yard was flat, not hilly like mine. He was playing with a red remote controlled car. It was shaped like a race car and had lightning stickers and bumpy black tires. I walked over.

He ran the car over a little jump made from a brick and some plywood boards. "Look," he said, "I just got it last night. It goes ten miles an hour for fifteen minutes straight without having to change the batteries."

"It can't go ten miles an hour if it only goes for fifteen minutes," I argued. "It'd have to go for an hour at least for that."

The car turned too fast and flipped over. Steven walked over and put it right side up. "Stupid. Ten miles an hour is how fast it goes. It doesn't matter how long."

I didn't say anything. I just watched Steven play with the car. He shot it off fast as he could one way down the sidewalk. Then he turned it and shot it off the other way.

"Freddy spent the night at his grandma's, but he'll be back soon. I'll get him to bring over those toy trucks his mom just bought him and we can make it jump them."

"You got it yesterday?"

"Yeah, I saved up my allowance." Steven stared at the car while he made it drive around. He switched and made it go backwards.

"I went out there this morning, but you weren't there."

"Yeah I was," he replied, still watching the car.

"I looked over from our corner and no one was down there. I even waved."

"I saw you. I waved back, but you left."

I hadn't seen anybody, but I must have been wrong. He'd been there. I should've walked all the way down. I was almost sure I hadn't seen anybody. "You didn't go?"

"Nah. I was going to, but figured I'd give you guys another chance."

"I didn't get chicken! I was there, I just went home when I didn't see you."

Steven ran the car to full speed and then ran it off the jump again. It flipped over, but then it tumbled and kept going. He just kept playing with the car.

# Keep Away

I t stunk. It was almost three and my dad was just turning back onto our block. He went to one of his meetings and made me go with because my mom took my sister to some dumb Campfire Girl thing and he said I couldn't stay home by myself.

There wasn't anything to do there, just wait outside the room where everybody talked for hours. I sat in the hard plastic chair with the metal legs and stared at stuff. The empty coffee pot with the brown gunk dried at the bottom. The gumball machine with only dried-up peanuts. The faded electric beer clock that hummed all loud.

Sunday was almost all gone and I hadn't done anything fun. The program people finally stopped talking, though, and my dad drove us home. Steven finished gluing his model stock car together and said I could help put the decals on. I thought maybe he hadn't done it yet. If I hadn't gone to my dad's meeting I could have helped cut the decals out, too.

"You make your bed?" My dad asked like he knew what I was thinking. "I didn't check, but you know I will sometime." He looked ahead at our street. Not at anything. There wasn't anything to look at. The block was empty, just a bunch of parked cars.

"Yes," I moaned, worried he'd make me do stuff and not let me go.

He nodded, though, still looking straight and not at me. Maybe that was all he could think of. Good thing I really made my bed instead of just pulling up the covers like usual. I bet he was going to go and check.

"Great," my dad said, kind of snarly. He didn't really mean it was great, though. I could tell. Whatever it was wasn't great.

My dad slowed our fake-wood station wagon, like he was going to park at the curb instead of in our driveway. He twisted his hands on the wheel like he was choking it. Then I saw Nicky coming at us, looking all dweeby and arms flapping everywhere, smiling like anybody liked him. He ran like a girl, only dorkier. He ran right down the street at us. He'd have run right into our station wagon if my dad hadn't stopped.

Stupid Nicky, he was such a pest. I didn't even like him. He was too little for anything, but he wouldn't leave me alone. If I tried to go to Steven's, he'd follow me everywhere and my dad would make me play with him. Because that was nice.

"Annoying prick," my dad mumbled, stopping the car. I guessed he didn't actually like him either. One time he told me Nicky was a hyper little S-word.

Nicky ran up to my dad's window. His curly brown hair was all nappy and sweaty, like his mom didn't comb it. That baby knew I didn't want to play with him so he'd ask my dad. Then I couldn't say no.

"Dumb old Nicky," I muttered. "I wish he'd go bug somebody else. Steven doesn't have to play with him."

My dad looked over at me, kind of weird. I thought maybe he was mad because I wasn't nice. He didn't look mad, though. He just stared at me, like he was thinking about something. Then he turned and unrolled his window, cranking the stiff metal handle by the swirly white cap on the end.

"Can Peter come out and play?" Nicky asked, acting like I wasn't even in the car. Dummy. I was sitting right there. I heard him.

"Peter is grounded," my dad snapped. I gaped at him. I hadn't done anything bad enough to get grounded. "He has to stay inside today so you'll have to go home, and don't run out in front of my car again or I'll spank you and then go tell your dad."

Nicky's face sank. That made him look even more like a dork. My dad rolled the window back up, hard, but Nicky just stood there. Finally, my dad pointed at Nicky's house, his arm twitching a little, so Nicky walked slowly down there. He walked all slumped over, like my dad really spanked him.

"He really needs a good beating," my dad whispered. "Just one, I swear." He shook his head and sighed. Then he stomped the gas pedal, turning the wheel, and we lurched up our driveway hill.

I watched Nicky trudge on the sidewalk back to his house. He was so stupid. He looked like a puppy that just peed on the floor. I wanted to kick him, but then I felt bad. That wasn't a nice thing to want.

I smiled, though, thinking how my dad told him off. It was Nicky's own fault. My dad wouldn't do that if he didn't deserve it. Nicky was always doing stuff like that and everybody hated it. It was good someone finally yelled at him.

Then I remembered what my dad said about grounding me. Maybe he grounded me because of what I said even though he didn't like Nicky either. I didn't say anything that bad, not bad enough for grounding. It wasn't fair, but I guessed that was okay. Getting grounded was worth it as long as Nicky got his. At least I didn't have to play with him.

But then my dad stopped halfway up the driveway hill. Right before the part where the driveway went between Mr. Pang's house and ours, before the back where our garage was. My dad shot Nicky a quick look. He was almost all the way to his house.

"Hurry up," my dad said, quiet but not, like he was whispering loud. "Now's your chance, before he sees and comes running back." He turned to me and then looked back at Nicky. I stared, confused. "Go!"

I flung open the car door and tried to jump. My seatbelt was still on, though, and it snapped me back. I pulled at the buckle. Finally, I got loose and jumped out, just in time to see Nicky running. He must have heard and figured it out.

"Now!" My dad yelled.

I took off running through our yard. I had to beat Nicky to Steven's house. I just had to. I'd have to play with him if I didn't because he wouldn't go away. He couldn't follow me if I got inside, though. Steven wouldn't let him. Nicky was just a little nerd anyway. I couldn't let Nicky beat me to Steven's. Not in a race. I ran down our hill and out into the street. Right down the grass so I wouldn't trip on our cement stairs. I got going really fast, coming down the hill like that.

"No-o!" Nicky howled. He knew my dad lied. He was running really fast, too, but he couldn't catch me. I was too fast. I ran as hard as I could.

I looked back for a second, just to see where he was. He ran out into the street, but he still hadn't even made it as far as Mrs. Bateman's house. I was way ahead.

Tears were all over his face—it was all mashed-up and red. His Ghostbusters t-shirt was even getting wet. He was bawling, really bawling, like I took his trike or something. He tilted his head back and pushed his chin forward as he ran, like maybe that'd keep his crying from running out all over. He couldn't run good like that, though. He flopped and flailed everywhere. He was being even dorkier than usual. There was no way he could catch me if he ran like that.

"Wait!"

He didn't have to cry, even if my dad tricked him. It wasn't like I wouldn't ever play with him again. I just wasn't going to play with him right then. He didn't have to be such a baby about it. I did feel kind of bad, though. Like I'd done something wrong even though I didn't. I just wanted to go play at Steven's. That wasn't bad.

I didn't stop running, though. It made me mad that he cried. I didn't hit him or anything. He should have found something else to do and let me play with Steven alone. I started wanting him to cry, just because he was crying. It was his fault, for being such a dumb little baby.

"Don't!" He wailed as he tried to keep running, tripping over his untied shoe laces.

I did, though. He was a baby so I treated him like one. I jumped onto Steven's porch steps and threw open the door. Nicky was still way behind.

# Training Part 1

"She just dropped her robe and stood there," I said, shifting a little on Steven's bed. "You could see her back. She looked naked."

"Yeah," Steven agreed. "You could tell she was really naked. Not just pretending."

"Then she just grabbed him."

"I wish they'd showed her from the front when she did that," Freddy chimed in. He was sitting on Steven's floor.

"I wish a girl would do that to me," I replied.

Steven got up off his bed and lay down on the floor. He held his head in his hands and propped it up by resting his elbows on the floor. I laid out on the bed, kind of in the same way.

Steven didn't have a whole lot in his room. There was the bed that was against one of the blue walls under the one little window. He always kept the shade down. The window looked out on the space between Steven's house and the next one, so I guess he just didn't see any reason to keep it open.

Other than the bed, there was just the desk where Steven was supposed to do homework, and a bookcase. Steven didn't really have any books, just a couple of his dad's old Marine Corps manuals. Mostly he kept plastic model planes and pinewood derby cars on the shelves. Those and all his stupid baseball trophies.

"Maybe she would've been facing us if we'd seen Teen Wolf at the movies," Freddy suggested. "Maybe they edited that for TV."

"I bet she was," Steven said. He began rubbing himself on the brown carpet. "I bet you could see everything."

Freddy leaned back a little away from Steven. "What're you doing?"

"It feels good." Steven laughed. His eyes were closed a little.

I started rubbing, too, on Steven's bed. I thought about the girl from the movie. She grabbed me.

Freddy looked at us. Then even he stretched out on the floor and started doing it. "Hey. It does feel good." He said it like he hadn't believed us.

Steven had his eyes all the way closed, grinning. "You'd see her boobs. You'd see it all."

"Yeah," I said quick to Freddy, pushing up a little off the bed, "and if you do it long enough something happens."

I'd done that. On the carpet in my room. There'd been this old movie on where this little guy hid some paper in his shirt. Some real sneaky pretty girl snuck her hand inside his shirt and was reaching all over inside there trying to get it. She tickled him, inside his clothes, grabbing for the paper. When I was lying on the floor in my underwear I thought about her doing that and rubbed.

"What happens?" Freddy asked.

"You finish," I guess. I started rubbing again.

"Finish?" Steven opened his eyes.

"Yeah." They didn't look like they got it. I thought about it. That's what it was, *finishing*.

"Just do it long enough until something happens," I finally said. "You'll see."

"We should practice," Steven said, getting up. "We need to be ready." He looked around at Freddy and me.

"Huh?" Freddy asked and sat up. I sat up too.

"For a girl, stupid." Steven rolled his eyes. "You got to practice for when it happens. I bet you don't even know how to kiss a girl."

Freddy crossed his arms. "I do, too. I know better than you."

"Show me then. Show me how you'd kiss a girl," he challenged.

"With you? That's gross!"

"It's just training! Just do it or admit you don't know how."

"Fine," Freddy snapped. He scooted over to Steven on the floor. He put his arms on Steven's shoulders, kind of like he was hugging him but didn't want to get too close. Then he closed his eyes and gave him a quick peck on the mouth.

"There. See?"

"That's not how you kiss a girl!" Steven got up on his knees. "That's how you kiss your mom. *This* is how you're supposed to kiss a girl."

Steven wrapped his arms around Freddy's neck and pulled him over so their chests were touching. Then he closed his eyes and kissed Freddy, opening his mouth. It looked funny because they were both boys. Then Steven let go and pushed him away.

"See? That's how you're supposed to do it. With tongues and stuff."

"I know," Freddy said. "If you were a girl I would've."

"Doesn't matter," Steven said, standing up. "You got to

train and be ready so you do it right. Otherwise you'll never get to make out with girls."

Then Steven came over and sat on the bed. I guess it was my turn. I made sure to do it like he said.

At first it was weird when I had my eyes open. He was right in my face and I smelled his deodorant. I closed my eyes, though, and then it was okay. It was supposed to be practice for kissing a girl so I didn't think about kissing Steven. I thought about kissing the girl from the movie. That was all right.

We stopped and Steven stood up. "He knows how to do it," he told Freddy.

"Like you know," Freddy argued. "You push your tongue too hard. They don't do that in the movies."

Steven shook his head. "That's the movies. Movies are just pretend and they make it look like it's real."

Freddy didn't say anything to that. He couldn't. Everybody knew movie kissing wasn't real. Nobody would make movies if they had to kiss somebody just because it was a movie.

"We should practice being naked, too," Steven said.

"Anybody can be naked," Freddy sneered. "I'm naked all the time when I take baths."

"Not naked like that," Steven insisted. "Naked *with* somebody. It's not the same."

So we all took our clothes off. Steven locked the door to his room first. It locked by pushing in the knob and turning till it clicked. There was a little hole on the other side of the door and the knob unlocked if someone stuck a nail or something in it.

Freddy had on tighty-whities. All of us had them, but Freddy still had his on.

"Come on," Steven told Freddy.

"Don't watch."

"We'll see in a second anyway. Who cares?"

Freddy shrugged. "Just don't watch."

We turned around. It was kind of different while people were looking. Even if nobody wanted to see. It was kind of exciting. That was weird, though, so I didn't think about it.

"Okay."

We turned back around. He'd taken them off. Our clothes were all in a pile on the floor and he was standing like me, kind of covering himself up. Freddy and me looked over at Steven. At his face.

"Now lay down," he told Freddy as he got on the bed. He stretched out, waiting.

Freddy stopped a minute, but then he walked over and lay down next to Steven. Steven rolled over so that they were touching. I just stood there.

Suddenly, Freddy jumped up off of the bed. "Eee ee eeh heeh," he squealed. He jumped back and forth and shook. "Our wieners touched!"

"See?" Steven sat up. "That's why you got to train. It'd be all over if you were in bed with a girl and did that."

I started walking over to the bed. It was my turn and I wasn't going to act all freaky like Freddy.

"Steven!"

We all looked up. It was Steven's dad. He called up from downstairs.

"Just a minute!" Steven yelled back.

We all ran over and started grabbing clothes and trying to throw them on. Steven and Freddy both grabbed the same pair of pants.

"Those are mine," Steven tried to yell at him quietly. "Yours are over there."

"Who cares? Just get dressed!"

"He'll know if we aren't wearing our own clothes," Steven snapped. "He saw what I wore this morning."

Freddy let go of the pants and grabbed for his own. I tried to hop into mine in one jump, but my leg got caught. I tripped and had to jump around so I didn't fall.

"Steven!" His dad shouted again. "You coming?"

"Yeah," Steven yelled back again.

We finally got our clothes on and ran out Steven's room and down the stairs. We stopped before we got to the bottom, out of breath. Steven's dad was waiting.

"Yeah, Dad?" Steven was in front. Me and Freddy were behind him on the stairs.

Steven's dad looked at us. He was a quiet guy. Always real calm. He was a cable man.

"Your mother called," he told Steven. "She said she was going to stop by home on her way to Target. If you want to go with, she said to be ready in about twenty minutes."

"That's okay, Dad." He put his hand on the banister. "I'll just stay here."

"All right, then." Steven's dad hooked his thumbs in the front pockets of his pants. "So…what're you boys doing up there?"

Steven shrugged. "Just playing."

Steven's dad nodded. "All right, then. Go on and get back to it." He turned and walked off into the kitchen.

\*\*\*\*\*

Steven stopped kissing. "You're much better at training than Freddy is," he said.

"Yeah?" I opened my eyes.

Steven smoothed his hair down where it was messed up from rolling around. "Yeah. You don't act all dorky and spaz out. It makes it weird when he does that."

I didn't think Steven trained with Freddy again after that one time. The only training we did was when only me and Steven were around.

"We're getting pretty good at that," he said. "We need to move on to something else."

"Like what?" There were only so many things we could do. Neither of us were girls.

He scooted up the bed and sat up a little. "Rub it. With your hand."

"What?" I sat up a little, too. "Girls don't have one of those. I don't need to practice that."

He put his hands on his knees. "It's practice for me."

I sat up all the way and scooted to the other end of the bed. That wasn't something Steven needed to practice. It didn't sound like training at all.

"I don't know," I said finally.

He threw up his hands like he was mad. "Fine, then. Don't. I thought you were getting really good at the simple stuff and you were ready for harder training. I guess you're not. I guess you can only handle the baby stuff."

"It's not that," I said quick. "It's just, well...I don't know."

He shook his head. "And here I was going to share my leftover Halloween candy with you because you were helping me. I was even going to help you practice, too. But, you don't want to. Some friend you are. I bet Freddy would."

"Wait," I said and scooted back over on the bed. "I'll do it. I just had to think about it a minute."

Steven had a bunch of butterscotches in his candy. The orange ones that come wrapped in the yellow plastic wrappers. I'd seen them. His parents didn't hide his candy either, they just let him have it. Mine only let me have a couple of pieces a day except after trick or treating. They said I was allergic.

"Okay," Steven said. "Do it."

He spread out and leaned back. I looked at it for a while, but I grabbed it when he started looking mad again.

His was different than mine. It was shorter, but fatter. The end was bigger and darker, almost more brown than purplish like mine was.

"Do it or don't," he said and I did it.

It was squishy but not. Closing my eyes didn't help at all. I couldn't pretend it was anything else.

I didn't know how long I was supposed to do it. I hoped only for a little bit. Suddenly, I felt it move and my hand was wet. I jumped up and Steven laughed.

"Ha! Me play joke. Me go pee-pee in your Coke."

I shook my hand.

"Hey! Don't get pee on my floor. That's gross." He whacked me one on the arm.

"You peed! Why'd you do that?"

He laughed again. "It was funny."

I got off the bed and started grabbing my clothes. It was bad enough already. I couldn't believe he did that. Steven was a dick.

"Hey, stop. Don't get pissy," he laughed again.

I kept grabbing my clothes. I found my underwear and put them on.

"Come on," he said. "I won't do it again." He grabbed a piece of candy off the desk next to the bed and tossed it to me. I had to drop my clothes to be able to catch it. It was a butterscotch.

## Burden of a Little Brother

"What's yours?" Nicky asked, looking up from his paper. We were at his house, down the block from mine. He was holding a green crayon to it, like he'd stopped in the middle of drawing. There were crayons scattered all over the carpet. Nicky had dumped out a whole big Crayola box on the floor. There were some sheets of paper, too. Some we'd drawn on already and some we hadn't.

"This one's going to be a guy called Maximum Headroom. He's going to have a huge head." I reached for a blue crayon so I could draw some big old veins bulging on Maximum's forehead.

Nicky seemed more interested in mine than the one he was working on. Maybe his wasn't any good, the dork. We needed to have some really good ones. If they weren't, then nobody would buy them. Mine was going to turn out bad if he watched and bugged me the whole time. It was bad enough that I could feel his little brother watching me.

"I'm going to call mine Slight Sal because he's little," Nicky offered, even though I didn't ask. Nicky started coloring some more.

It still felt like his little brother was looking at me but I didn't want to check. He was standing over by us. I couldn't stop thinking about those fish eyes pushing out of his frog face. He'd be drooling, I was sure of that. His mouth hanging open. His jaw tugging down the pasty dough of his face, raw like it was cold even though it wasn't. Dim unblinking eyeballs. Like jelly. It made me feel sick, but it was bad to feel like that.

"How're you going to draw that?" I demanded, suddenly frustrated.

"Huh?"

47

"If you draw him full-sized no one will be able to tell he's supposed to be small, but if you draw him real small then most of the card will be blank. It won't work. People got to be able to tell what's wrong with him."

Nicky looked down at his paper. "Maybe I can make mine Silly Sal," he offered. "He can just look stupid." He looked over at his brother.

For the longest time I hadn't even known Nicky had a brother and I only lived a couple of houses down. One day Nicky's parents were just walking him down the sidewalk in front of their house. That was the first I'd ever seen him.

I thought maybe he'd been in the hospital for a long time, or had to be kept inside. He had this big scar on his chest I saw once when Nicky's mom took his shirt off and I'd heard something about operations. My parents said he had down syndrome. They told me I wasn't supposed to say anything about it.

"We're going to make lots of money, aren't we?" Nicky was looking up at me again.

"Sure. Everybody wants these. Topps has got to need more ideas. They can only come up with so many."

I reached for a purple crayon. I was going to add it to the veins so it'd look like Maximum's head was really throbbing. Nicky's little brother lunged and snatched it.

"No!" Nicky screamed and jumped up.

His little brother staggered back. He blinked and clutched the crayon. It reminded me of a turtle wanting to pull back into its shell, scared by a barking dog.

"Give it back," Nicky yelled, snatching away the crayon.

"*Aaghh!*" His little brother protested and shook his arms.

"Go away!" Nicky shoved.

He didn't need to do that. I would have just got another.

His little brother windmilled his arms, tipped over, and sat down. "*Ahhaagh!*" He flailed his arms and shook his head. He stopped, blinking again, as Nicky walked away. Nicky threw the crayon back on the pile and sat back down to work on his paper. "*Hhkss,*" his little brother spat.

I looked over at Nicky's little brother quick as I listened to hear if Nicky's mom was going to do anything. I thought she'd yell, too, telling us not to be mean. Cooking sounds still came from the kitchen. It was only through the dining room, though, so she couldn't have missed the yelling. Maybe she'd heard but just ignored it.

Nicky's little brother stood up once nothing was going on. He looked at the crayons again, but didn't go for them. Nicky went back to his paper.

His little brother looked away. Suddenly, he barreled over to the entertainment center Nicky's dad had built into the wall at the far end of the room. There was a little Big Bird tape player on one of the shelves underneath the TV, and he grabbed it. He pushed a button and Ernie from Sesame Street started singing the rubber ducky song.

"*Waahhkss. Wehks. Wehk,*" he aped the quacking on the tape, bubbling spit in his throat. He shifted from one foot to the other, holding the tape player, and turned slow circles. It was dancing, I suppose.

He moved around between the built-in shelves and the wood-burning stove in the corner. Nicky's parents used the big old black metal thing to heat the house sometimes when it was cold. I'd heard that Nicky's little brother hurt himself real bad on it one time. He'd been climbing, not knowing any better that he shouldn't touch it when it was hot. He got burns all up and down his arms and legs. I couldn't figure out how he'd gotten burned that much. I thought he'd stop touching it once it hurt him. It was warm out, though, and there was no fire going.

"Maybe we should get all the *Garbage Pail Kids*," Nicky suggested. "Then we could see what they already have. Get some ideas, too."

I shrugged. "I don't have any money. Maybe they've got a list they'd send us if we said we were working on new cards." I set Maximum on the pile of finished drawings and got a new piece of paper.

"Maybe they'd send us some cards to give us ideas," Nicky suggested hopefully.

"Maybe," I agreed, excited at the idea.

"What're you going to do with your money?"

"I'm going to finally get He-Man's Castle Greyskull. I asked for it for Christmas, but I never got it. Maybe I could get the He-Man sword too, the one that's big enough to really fight with," I continued, "and maybe even a TV for my room."

"Yeah, I'll get that, too," Nicky agreed. "Then I'm going to buy all the G.I. JOE's."

The tape player stopped and Nicky's little brother stopped dancing. He left the tape player by the wood-burning stove. As he wandered off, he walked right through where we were working and stepped on Nicky's paper. Nicky's crayon broke under his foot.

"Cut it out," Nicky yelled, jumping and pushing his little brother again. His little brother stumbled back again from being pushed, but stayed up this time.

"*Ahh! Hhkss.*" More spit bubbles. He shook his head. It almost looked like he was arguing with Nicky about it.

"Mom!" Nicky yelled to his mom in the kitchen. "Little Peter won't leave us alone!"

Nicky's little brother was named Peter, too. They called him Little Peter so they wouldn't confuse him with me. Like how Nicky and his dad were little Nick and big Nick. I didn't like it, though. They couldn't mix him up with me.

Nicky's mom walked in from the kitchen and looked at us. She was wearing a bathrobe and her hair was all messy, like she hadn't combed her hair after she got up. "Let him play with you, Nicky."

"He's messing up our Garbage Pail Kid Cards," Nicky wailed.

"Oh, no one's going to buy those, anyway. He's not hurting anything."

"Yes they will," Nicky argued. "They'll buy them and make them into cards. You'll see." Little Peter tried to pick up a crayon and Nicky smacked his hand. "No! Leave it alone," Nicky shouted at him.

"Nicky," his mother sighed, "he just wants to play with you boys."

"I don't care," Nicky snapped. "He always messes everything up. I hate him. I wish he hadn't been born."

I flinched. Nicky's mom was going to get mad. "Nicky," I piped up, "you shouldn't be mean. You never know. He could grow up and be rich and then he might not share."

"No he won't. He's just a dummy." Nicky kicked the empty crayon box.

I looked at Nicky's mom quick. "He could. I heard him quacking just like the tape. Maybe he'll do impressions and get famous."

Nicky's mom shook her head. She looked tired. "Peter, Little Peter won't become famous for impressions. You aren't being realistic."

I remembered one time she told Little Peter to set the table. He did it, too. I couldn't believe it. He couldn't even talk. Nicky's mom seemed surprised that I didn't think he could do chores and I felt bad. Then there was this.

"If you don't want Little Peter bothering you, then go play in your room," Nicky's mom told him. "You have to accept that he's going to try to play too if you stay out here."

Nicky grumbled, but started upstairs. His mom went back in the kitchen. The crayons and Garbage Pail Kid cards were left in the piles. I guessed we weren't doing that anymore. Even Little Peter didn't seem interested in them.

Nicky's room had a latch so he could keep Little Peter out. It was one of those hook and eye things people put on screen doors. Nicky closed the door.

"You want to play Star Wars?" He pointed at the heap of action figures all over his bed.

"Do you have the Han Solo carbonite set?" I really wanted that after I saw the commercial. It was really cool. A little Han Solo went in one side and a cast metal block, gold-colored, came out the other. The block even had Han Solo popping out, covered in metal. I'd asked for that for Christmas, too, but hadn't gotten it either.

"Yeah, but I can't find frozen Han so it isn't any good to play with."

"Oh," I responded, disappointed both that I couldn't play with it and that it didn't do anything but switch Hans. I thought it did something cool to make a frozen one.

"You know," I said, perking up and sifting through the action figures, "you ought to keep these good. The originals are worth a bunch of money now."

"Yeah!" Nicky beamed. "Everyone else will probably break them playing. If we don't, then when everybody else's break, we'll have the only ones. We'll be rich!"

"You just have to take care of them."

"I've got a case," Nicky replied, digging around in his closet. He started throwing toys all over his room. He pulled what looked like a huge Dark Vader head lunchbox out of the mess. "Here it is!"

"Yeah, keeping them in a case is smart."

Nicky ran over to the bed. The case had all sorts of plastic dividers inside making hundreds of tiny little boxes, each just big enough for a figure. Nicky started grabbing from the pile and stuffing the case. I just watched. He was the one that made the mess. Let him clean it up.

"There," he said, closing it. "Now we just got to put them away until they're worth money."

I didn't say anything. That would probably take a long time. Like a year at least.

"So, what do you want to do?" Nicky asked after a couple of minutes. Trying to make money off toys getting collectible wasn't as much fun as making Garbage Pail Kid cards. There just wasn't much to do.

"I don't know."

Nicky looked around. "Hey! Maybe Little Peter has toys that could be worth money someday."

"He might," I agreed.

"We should go check. He won't know to take care of them. We should put them up for him. Then we can sell them when they're rare."

"Won't he notice they're gone?" It seemed kind of mean to take his toys.

"Nah," Nicky shook his head. "He doesn't even know what he has. He won't miss anything once it's gone. It's a waste to let him play with stuff and ruin it. Come on."

I followed. Little Peter's room was right across the hall from Nicky's. It was creepy and smelled kind of funny. The walls were this dark thick yellow. Dried mustard. The bed, next to a tiny plastic dresser, didn't have a headboard or anything. The room was pretty clean, though. There were only a few toys in the corner, stuff like a Grover doll.

"There isn't much," I said.

"Let's check the closet."

The closet was right next to the door. It must have shared a wall with Nicky's closet. It was bigger than Nicky's, though. We could've both stood inside if it wasn't for all the toys. There was a big shelf, too.

"See anything?" Nicky asked, pawing through the toys and tossing them out into the room.

I grabbed something. It was a play dashboard. It had a steering wheel and a horn that could honk. "I don't think anybody would pay money for this stuff," I muttered. "Nobody's going to collect it."

"Yeah," Nicky agreed. "It's all baby stuff."

We kept looking, though, and Nicky kept throwing all the toys into the middle of the room. It was getting pretty messy. Soon we'd emptied the closet. We'd kind of trashed the room, too. If Nicky was going to take his little brother's stuff, he could at least not make a mess of his room.

"Hey," Nicky noted once the closet was empty, "we could use this as a clubhouse. It's perfect without anything in it. Secret."

"There's no chairs, though."

"We'll sit on the shelf. It's strong. My dad built it."

Nicky closed the closet door and we scrambled up onto the shelf. It wasn't easy, the shelf was pretty high, but we made it. Just a little light came in from Little Peter's room so we could see.

Nicky was right, it felt secret in the empty closet. No one could see us. I thought about how we could make a secret passage into Nicky's closet. That way we could come and go without anybody knowing. Maybe there was even a secret passage already.

Light poured in as the closet door tore open. Both Nicky and I jerked back.

"*Hhkss*," Little Peter bubbled his spit. He'd flung the door open. Him with his fish eyes and doughy cheeks. He tried to come in, but Nicky kicked him back with his foot.

"*Hhhhuks!*" Little Peter flailed his arms all around. He started smacking his face and pulling on his hair. "*Aahhh!*"

Nicky kicked him back again and then leaned down and pulled the door shut. Little Peter got it open, but Nicky quickly shut it again. Then he held it closed. It wasn't right for Nicky to kick his little brother like that. It was Little Peter's closet, after all. I didn't say anything, though. I didn't really want him in there with us either.

"*Guhhaaaaa!*" Little Peter screamed on the other side of the closet door. He started banging. Loud. He kept pulling on the door and hitting it. I heard him smacking his head some more, too.

I thought for sure Nicky's mom heard and would come up to yell at us. She didn't, though. We just sat in there on the shelf. Nicky kept holding the door shut and Little Peter kept banging, trying to get in.

I didn't see why he wanted in so bad. All his toys were in the middle of his room by then. Maybe he thought we were hiding stuff from him even though he saw the closet was empty. Maybe he just didn't understand.

# Training Part 2

"**T**his'll be perfect," I told Nicky.

He came walking up into the lookout fort behind me. It was on a high part of the hill of the graveyard. There was a big flat area so there was plenty of room to sit and there were a bunch of trees so people down on the street couldn't see in. No one'd see us kissing anybody.

"Yeah," Nicky agreed. He held up a couple pillows he'd dragged along. They were big and overstuffed. Dark brownish-green with designs all over them. "My mom said we could have these for it."

"You told your mom we were going to have a kissing booth?"

"Sure." He tossed the pillows down on the ground. There were two of them. We each sat on one.

"Do you think a lot of girls will come?"

"I bet they will," I told him. "Kissing booths always get lots of people."

We'd made a sign with magic marker that had an arrow up to us and taped it to a tree at the bottom of the hill. All we had to do was wait for the girls.

It was a great idea. We didn't know why everybody else didn't open kissing booths. Girls just came to kiss. We wouldn't even have to try to talk them into it. Maybe other people would do it, too, once they saw how well it worked for us.

"So how much should we charge?" Nicky asked after a while.

"Charge?"

"Yeah, don't people have to pay? Like a dollar a kiss or something?"

I threw a stick at him. "Dummy! You're not going to kiss a girl because she doesn't want to pay a dollar? If we charge we might not get as many!"

"Oh," Nicky chewed on his lip. "Maybe we should at least charge the ugly ones, though."

"Good idea. Kisses are free but if the girl's gross she has to pay a dollar."

Nicky looked down at the alley. There was nobody down there. There was nobody down our block either. It was Sunday and it was pretty quiet.

"Do you think it'll just be kissing? Maybe they'll let us do other stuff, like see their boobs?"

"Sure," I shrugged. "If they come to kiss somebody they'll probably neck or something like that."

That made me think about Heather. I was always staring at her during class. She never talked to me, though, so I didn't think she'd let me kiss her or anything. Thinking about necking made me think about necking with Heather. I got really wound up thinking about that.

No girls were coming, though. We had a sign up, but nobody was coming. There wasn't even anybody walking by. We'd waited for a while, too. Maybe even an hour.

"Maybe we should practice until we get some girls," I suggested. I'd still been thinking about Heather. "Like training."

"Naw," Nicky replied.

"No?"

"I want to kiss *girls*. Not you."

I grabbed another stick and threw it at him. "Stupid! This is just while there aren't any girls. If there were girls, we wouldn't kiss each other."

He threw the stick back, but not hard. It didn't even come close to me.

"But I don't want to," he replied.

"Tell you what," I bargained. "If you let me practice necking, then you get first pick of any girl that comes to the booth. I'll even kiss the ugly ones myself if I have to."

His eyes opened wide. Then they narrowed a little. "Just today, or all the time?"

"All the time."

"What if they want to kiss you and not me?"

"Then they have to kiss you first or I won't do it," I promised. "It isn't even a big deal. Steven does it."

"All right," he sighed and tilted his head to one side. "But just until girls show up."

"Right," I agreed, pulling my pillow next to his.

"You don't get to keep all the money we make either," he said, "even if you do kiss all the ugly girls."

"I don't care," I said. Then I closed my eyes. I was going to neck with Heather.

*****

"See? It's like a girl," Nicky told me.

I tried it like Nicky said. He'd wanted to do that so he had me try it. He was going to do it next.

"It is, kind of," I said, even though Nicky didn't have boobs. None of the girls in my class really had boobs yet either, though.

"Told you."

We were in Nicky's bed, but we were only kind of naked. If Nicky's parents called, we had to be able to get dressed fast. They'd get suspicious if we didn't come right away. All the way naked would take too long. We took our shirts off but kept them close by. We didn't take our pants all the way off either. We just pulled them down so they'd be easy to pull up again. The blankets were over us. Nobody could see that we were doing anything, but it'd look weird if they saw us in the bed.

"Maybe for the sleepover I can get one of my mom's bras," he suggested. "That'd be even better."

"We'd have to put something in it," I replied, "or it wouldn't stay on."

He shrugged.

The sleepover wasn't for another week. Nicky'd begged his parents for forever before they let him have one, probably because his little brother acted up when people came over. They finally said yes.

We'd been planning the sleepover for a month. Nicky talked about it all the time. At the sleepover we wouldn't have to be so careful. His parents wouldn't check on us so much. We'd even be fully naked in the bed and not have to worry about them.

"My turn," Nicky said.

I rolled over on my back. I didn't think he was doing it right. I didn't say anything, though. I didn't have to teach him anything. As long as I got to practice the right way he could do it wrong all he wanted.

"I saw Mrs. Bateman's boobs," he said. "That's what these are."

"No you didn't, Nicky," I snapped. "You're lying."

Mrs. Bateman was his next-door neighbor. She moved in with her husband a couple of months before. They had a hound dog they kept in the backyard. She was fat and had red hair, but she did have big boobs.

"She did so. She was getting undressed and I saw her through the window. She saw me looking."

"Stop lying, Nicky. She wouldn't do that."

It was dumb that Nicky lied. I didn't even want to see Mrs. Bateman's boobs. They'd be gross. If he was going to lie he could at least lie and say he saw Steven's sister's boobs. That'd be worth lying about.

"Nicky?" His mom knocked on the door. "It's time for dinner. Peter needs to go home."

I jumped out of the bed and pulled my pants up. Nicky tried to do the same, but he got caught in the blanket. I pulled on my shirt. I took care of myself first before worrying about Nicky.

"Coming, Mom," he tried to say while wrestling with the blankets. "We're coming."

He needed to hurry. She wasn't calling from downstairs. She was right outside the door. I bet she could hear us.

"Nicky, I—" She stopped, standing in the open doorway.

Nicky was so stupid! He hadn't latched the door. She wouldn't have even asked why it was latched. He always latched it so his little brother couldn't get in. He hadn't this time, though, and she'd just walked right on in.

His mom stared. I looked down at myself. I didn't look like anything. My clothes were all on and I was just standing next to the bed. She was looking at Nicky, though. He'd gotten loose of the blanket, but he was still in the bed. His shirt was off and his pants were around his ankles. Me looking okay didn't help if he looked like that.

She just stood there for a couple minutes. Her face looked like it was frozen. Nicky and I didn't move either. Then, her face started twisting all up. Her mouth clamped shut.

"Peter," she finally said with her teeth gritted. "Go downstairs. *Now.*"

I tried to go, but she was still in the door. She almost seemed frustrated when I went to get around her. It was like she didn't think I had to go through the door to get downstairs. Finally, she moved enough to get by. She shuddered. Nicky was still lying on the bed.

I ran downstairs as soon as I got around her. I wanted to get out of there as fast as I could. Let Nicky get the worst of whatever she was going to do, I figured. I almost ran right out the door. I thought she'd probably call my parents, though, before I got home if I didn't do what she said. I sat down on the couch and waited.

Still, I thought she would've yelled or smacked us or something. I couldn't hear them, but it didn't seem like she was doing anything like that. Maybe we weren't in that much trouble. Maybe she'd just tell us not to do it anymore.

Nicky's cabbage patch kid was sitting on the couch next to me and I picked it up. It was mostly bald with just a little bit of black hair in the middle of its head. Nicky named it Guido even though cabbage patch kids came already named.

I had nothing to do, waiting there. The cabbage patch kid had lips so I practiced kissing those. It didn't work good. The lips were hard plastic and I couldn't really kiss them.

"Peter," Nicky's mom snapped, walking down the steps. I tossed the doll away. Nicky wasn't with her.

"Yes?" I tried to slouch so it looked like I felt really sorry. Maybe she wouldn't punish me if I looked like I already felt bad enough.

She stopped in front of the couch. Her face was still all twisted. It kept twitching. She didn't look like I was in trouble, but almost like I was covered in dog doo. She kept almost saying something, but then stopping herself again before she actually talked.

"Peter," she finally stammered. "We don't do that in this house." She said 'that' real loud.

She stopped. I didn't say anything.

"It's wrong. The bible says that it is."

I knew that stuff from Sunday school. God didn't want people making out with anybody if they weren't married. It wasn't *doing it*, though, so it wasn't as bad. I didn't tell her I knew it was bad. Maybe I wasn't in as much trouble because she thought I didn't know any better.

"I want you to leave," she said, her face still twitching. "There will be no sleepover. I don't think Nicky should play with you so much for a while either."

I didn't get it. She didn't yell or call my parents. She just kept looking at me like I had puke all over me. Then I got it. She wasn't talking about people making out. But we weren't doing that. Steven wasn't like that. That was gross. This was just training. That's all. I wasn't like that either.

"I want you to leave right now," she said and pointed at the door.

I got up quick. She opened the door and I ran out. After I went through, she slammed it.

# Boys Chase Girls

I walked down the block past that little dork Nicky's house. I was on my way up to the hill by the graveyard to my new fort. It was really cool. My friend Steven didn't make this one. It was all mine. Steven always got to make the forts. Then, when he was mad, he'd say I couldn't go in them. He couldn't do that with this one, though, because it wasn't his.

I built it with all these foam boards I'd found in the trash after one of my neighbors put siding on their house. They were big and flat, like life-size sticks of gum that comes with baseball cards. It wasn't squishy foam either. It was stiff. The fronts and backs were coated in foil, with all these tiny black letters printed all over it, squishing the blue foam in between. They looked like ice cream sandwiches astronauts might eat. I took all of them. Trash meant nobody wanted them anyway.

Hidden way on the top of the hill by the graveyard's chain link fence, on a high spot surrounded by a half circle of little trees, that was where I built it. I jammed the foam boards between the trees and fence to make walls and a roof, like a shiny metal box. It wasn't that big, though; I had to crouch down inside, but even Steven's forts didn't have roofs. I made doors, too. A front one and a back one so I could escape to either side. It was the best fort. I even covered it with branches and leaves so nobody'd see it from the alley.

I walked across the broken-up old asphalt of the alley to get to my fort, back on the part of the alley between my block and the next, but when I get there my fort's all broken!

There were little broken up bits of foam and foil all over the hill. Even down in the potholes in the alley. No piece bigger than a quarter. The half circle of little trees were all bent and mashed, too, leaves and branches ripped off. It looked bare. I saw everything from the alley. I didn't even have to go up the hill to look. I just stared. Then I heard somebody whisper, "Shhh. Come on."

I looked toward the noise. Three girls were tiptoeing down the path on the hill, looking away all casual through the fence into the graveyard like I wouldn't see them if they did. I'd never seen them before. They all had the same brown hair, but different. The first girl, the one with long hair, was almost as tall as me. She had on a billowy green skirt and this weird slick red jacket that was shiny like plastic. It looked more like a costume than clothes, but not like it was actually supposed to be anything. Costumes are supposed to be something. A shorter, chunkier, curly-haired girl was in the middle. The last was a real little kid with long, long hair. Down to her waist. They were sneaking away from my fort!

"Hey!" I yelled. They looked down at me, watery eyes all big and staring. All three of them, frozen like squirrels in the road right when they first see my dad's car coming at them. Then the first girl twitched like she was going to keep running. "Hey!" I yelled again. "What're you doing up there?!"

They unfroze and ran away. All three of them in a line. Like Goldilocks, but backwards, and they were the bears. Tallest to shortest. They were running because they wrecked my fort! "Come back here!" I ran down the alley after them. "I'll kill you!"

They ran faster away from me on the hill. They didn't even look back. I ran faster, too. "I'll catch you," I kept yelling as I ran. "You're going to be sorry!"

I ran really fast, but they were already pretty far ahead. The alley was full of potholes so I couldn't really run straight. Big ones, rough and full of gross old water. Even dodging around I kept stepping in one and tripping, twisting up my ankle. There were rocks all over the place I had to miss, too. The girls just got further away and I started getting tired. They didn't seem to be slowing down at all, though. Then I stopped because my side started hurting real bad and I couldn't run anymore.

"I'm going to find you!" I tried to shout, but it was hard to breathe. I had to hold my side just to be able to talk. "You can't hide!"

*****

She couldn't hide, the first girl I mean. Not for long.
She started going to my school. Not in my class, but I saw her
when they mixed the fifth grade classes for stuff. She must have
just moved and changed schools so that was why I hadn't seen
her before. I didn't even have to look for her. She was just there.
Still, I couldn't just get her, not in class. I had to wait for my
chance.

"Come on," I muttered, fidgeting impatiently next to a
metal pole.

We were all at the football field. Not at school, my
school didn't have a football field. The school had taken all the
fifth grade classes to the college for track and field. Everybody
had just gotten done eating lunch and were running around on
the fake grass some before the teachers got everybody back on
the buses. There was a black spongy track, all covered in painted
lines and numbers, running all around the field. It looked like
cork but was all rubbery and smelled like plastic. Joy was walking
circles around the field on it, by herself.

That was her name, *Joy*. One of the girls in her class
told me. The girl said nobody in class liked Joy because she was
weird. Joy told the other girls her dad had these really old
Crayola bears he kept in a secret room hidden in their basement.
Supposedly all sorts of people wanted them so they were worth
like ten thousand dollars each and Joy said her dad was going to
give them to her when she grew up.

Nobody believed her.

"Keep walking," I whispered, gripping the metal pole
so hard my arm twitched. I couldn't get her when there were
teachers around. Joy knew it and acted like I wasn't even there. I
outsmarted her, though.

There were these big metal bleachers at one end
between the field and the track. Almost as tall as my house.
Rows of flat metal benches going from the top all the way down

to the ground and flat metal bars crisscrossing all around and bolted to each other inside. Like they were a giant Erector Set. I snuck behind them. The teachers were all in the middle of the field, jawing. When Joy walked around the bleachers on the track, they couldn't see her anymore.

It seemed like I'd waited forever. I thought maybe she'd figured it out, but then she came walking around, looking at some stupid butterfly. She had on a white jean skirt, her hair tied back in a ponytail for track and field, and canvas shoes. Not tennis shoes. They were like Keds, but not real Keds. She wouldn't run fast wearing those. Not faster than me with my new high-top Pony shoes. They had square bumps on the bottoms for digging into dirt. I don't know why she was wearing that stuff on track and field day. She was dumb.

I stayed put until she walked a little past. When I couldn't make myself wait anymore, I jumped out. Joy heard me and spun around. She froze, arms out, crouched down a little. Feet spread apart like she was leading off to steal a base. Her eyes open wide. She looked like a squirrel in the road again, so that made me my dad's car. She turned and bolted right before I started running. Her ponytail bobbed around all over the place as she ran.

"I got you now! You're going to get it," I yelled as I chased her. She didn't say anything back. She just ran. She ran faster than me when I yelled and ran at the same time so I stopped yelling. Then I started catching up.

Suddenly, right as I was about to grab her, she ducked under the bleachers and ran in and out of the metal poles. I followed and tried to keep running as fast while dodging around, but I smacked right into the pole. I'd run on one side of a pole but didn't pull my wrist around with me. Full speed. The bleachers sounded like they were about to fall, a big hollow metal noise. My arm was on fire. "Aaghh!"

I tried to keep running, but my arm throbbed so bad I couldn't run right. It hurt from my shoulder all the way to my fingers, even though I'd only hit my wrist. I fell behind quick. I worried my arm was probably broke and I'd have to tell my parents how I did it. I'd have to think of something to tell them.

Joy didn't stop at all, not even to look and laugh. She had to have heard it.

\*\*\*\*\*

I kicked a hole in the dirt under the gravel on the playground. A couple of kids climbed around on the unpainted metal jungle gym next to me. A little ways off a bunch of black kids that got bussed to my school played basketball on the blacktop. The hoop was bent and didn't have a net anymore.

They hadn't let us out for recess for a while. There was no recess in winter, but they started letting us out a little after the track meet. Then it rained really hard for weeks. If it rained or was too muddy they sent us back to class after lunch and made us play board games and stuff. That wasn't too bad. There was one game where we were police chasing a crook and there was this remote we got to push buttons on to see if we caught him where we landed. The rain had finally stopped, though, and the ground dried so they let us outside again.

I'd made a game of making Joy run all the time. The whole fifth grade had recess at the same time every day so we were always both there when there was recess. The monitors didn't pay much attention. She couldn't just go where I wasn't. She had to keep running.

"Joy!" I took off running suddenly, seeing her. She was wearing a baggy old gray sweatshirt, like it was big enough for an adult, with something about a fun run written on it. She also had on a long brown skirt, long enough to be a dress, and shiny black plastic shoes. "Get over here! You're just making it worse!"

She ran, eyes bugging out for a second when she saw me. That was good. I was keeping her frightened and jumpy. That way, she'd never enjoy recess. Actually getting her would end the fun.

"I'm catching up," I called after her. I was careful not to slow down because I yelled so she didn't get away. She didn't look back, hopefully because she worried I was right behind her and she'd really get it if she even turned around to look. I couldn't be sure, though, since I couldn't see her face.

"Go away," she shouted back. She ran off to the side and kept running like that until I was chasing her back toward the jungle gym. There was only so much space for her to run. She couldn't go outside the playground fence. If she didn't double back like she did, I'd trap her.

"I'm going to get you today," I taunted her when we got near the jungle gym.

"Stop!" She frantically circled around the jungle gym. I circled, too. A couple fourth-graders on top just watched us run around them. They didn't look like it was a big deal.

Joy wasn't running fast enough. She looked like she was trying, but it was too easy to keep up with her. Those black plastic shoes were no good for running. I kept slowing myself down so she wouldn't figure out I wasn't really trying to grab her. Not right then at least. She had to think I was serious or she wouldn't run and it wouldn't be any more fun.

For a couple minutes she just ran around and around the jungle gym. The fourth-graders weren't even looking at us anymore. Suddenly, Joy broke away and ran off onto the blacktop.

"Don't let him get me," she cried, running right through the basketball game. She surprised a short black kid with a fade who had the ball. It flew off and rolled away. The black kids looked mad, but she ran through them too quick. A couple of them pushed me, when I ran through after her though I ignored the push and kept running. They weren't helping her. A couple of pushes was nothing.

That fat, mean kid Rodney stepped right out between me and Joy. "Hey," he said. "What do you think you're doing?" I almost ran into him because he jumped in there so quick. I stopped so I didn't run into him before I had a chance to think what I was doing. Joy stopped, too, looking back like she wanted to see what was going on.

"Getting her," I said, pointing and moving quick to run around him at Joy. Joy squealed and ran the other way so Rodney was still in between us. Not that it was hard. Rodney was really fat. Everybody said his dad sent him to fat camp last summer.

"Cut it out," he said and pushed me hard in the chest. It kind of stung. Rodney was fat, but he was strong too. "She's a girl."

"She wrecked my fort!" I screamed, more around him to Joy than to him.

"No I didn't!" She hid behind Rodney, peeking over. "My little sister did. Nadine broke it playing karate. We didn't even know it was anything, we just thought it was some trash stuck in some trees. We didn't think anybody would mind."

Rodney crossed his arms over his blubber. "See? She didn't even do anything."

Rodney made me mad. He pretended he was nice and wanted to help her, but I knew he didn't. He thought it was funny to do stuff like stick chewed gum in people's hair or hit them for flinching. Even girls. All he had to do was be mean to me and Joy'd think he was nice. He probably hoped she'd like him, even though she wouldn't because he was so fat. He got to be the nice guy and still got to be a bully at the same time.

"She's still going to pay," I shouted, running around him at her again.

"No!" He grabbed my arm hard and twisted. Joy hid behind him, making sure he stayed between us. "I said you can't touch her." He twisted really hard, like he wanted it to hurt, smiling–not like he wanted to protect Joy. He barely even let go when I stopped trying to get her and stomped off. My arm was all red.

"You okay?" I heard him ask her. I knew he was grinning, thinking how funny it was that he'd made me mad.

I walked a little ways away and watched them from the green monkey bars. She talked to him for a bit, but Rodney was a dork. Sooner or later, I knew she'd get sick of talking to him and wander off. Then I'd get her. I didn't even really want to get her anymore. That's what was so stupid about Rodney. I just wanted to mess with her a little, make her run. He wasn't really saving her from anything.

Sure enough, I waited long enough and Joy started walking around on her own again. I sneaked closer. When I got as close as I could, I charged. She saw me and ran right for the center of the blacktop again, right behind Rodney! I didn't really even get to chase her. I bet they'd planned the whole thing.

"I told you to leave her alone!" He held up a big ham of a fist, getting ready to swing. *He was really going to beat me up!* I thought. I tried to think quick. I had to get myself out of this or Rodney was going to pound me.

"Wait," I said, breathing hard. This wasn't any good anyway. It wasn't any fun pretending I was going to kill her if I couldn't chase her around. She'd just always hide behind Rodney, never scared because she'd always be safe. "I'm not trying to get her."

"No?" Rodney smiled all cross-eyed, like he was pretending to be stupid and believe me even though he didn't.

"I want a truce," I said. "If you won't break my forts again I won't get you and we can forget it. Be friends."

"Really?" Joy peeked out from behind Rodney. Her eyes brightened and she smiled a little, pulling her long brown hair out of her face. It'd kind of gotten messed up from all the running.

"Sure," I said, even though I'd just said the first thing that came to mind. I suppose it was a pretty good idea, thinking about it. If I couldn't chase her, this was the next best thing. Someone else to hang out with. She was a girl and all, too.

# Druthers Part 1

"This is the foxhole fort," I told my friend Joy.

We were on the hill by the graveyard. Joy's sister, Jeanie, and Jeanie's friend, Courtney, were there, too. They weren't important, though. I told Joy I'd show her our forts since she'd just moved in. Jeanie and Courtney had come, too, but just because they didn't have anything better to do. Jeanie kept not paying attention and just followed along, bored. Courtney watched real careful, even though she kept hanging back with Jeanie. I couldn't tell if she was bored or not.

Joy leaned and looked down in. When that little twerp, Nicky, and me, found the place, it'd been just a little ravine in the hill, all crumbling so I kept falling in. We'd dug it out so we could stand inside and peek out at people driving down the alley. I was standing inside. Jeanie and Courtney were keeping back. Jeanie smacked the gum she was chewing.

"What's it going to be when it's done?" Joy asked, fixing her headband to keep her long brown hair back more.

I looked at her. "It's done now. It's a foxhole."

"Oh." She stood up.

"Okay, you've showed it to her, Peter," Jeanie complained, frowning. Her face was just ordinary normally, but it made me think of a grumpy old man when she frowned. "Let's get going already."

I put my hands on the side and heaved myself up, getting dirt on my pants. It was dusty not muddy, though, so I just took a second to brush it off. Jeanie muttered something to Courtney and Courtney put her hand over her mouth and laughed, looking at me. I didn't know what that was all about.

"The lookout fort is over this way," I told Joy, starting off on the path along the chain link graveyard fence. Joy followed me.

"Careful," I said, looking over at Joy. We were at the spot where the hill had washed away almost all the way to the fence. It made a steep kind of slide down to the alley with just a little bit to walk on up at the top. We usually just ran real fast so we'd get across before we started to slide down, but I didn't think the girls could do that. They all had skirts on, too. "You got to hold onto the fence," I told them.

I ran to the other side like normal and then I held out my hand so I could help Joy across, in case she slipped. She held onto the fence, though, and stepped sideways across the path okay. Then she walked around me and waited out of the way. Jeanie just stomped across, grabbing the fence a couple of times when she slipped. She even made a bored face while she went across like it was no big thing. Courtney didn't start stepping over at first. She looked at me and then down at the slide, like she was pretending to be scared.

"Come on!" Jeanie rolled her eyes.

"All right!" She started across, but made a big show of grabbing tight onto the fence. Then she inched over little bit by little bit, even though she had room to stand. It was funny. They were girls, but it wasn't that big of a slope. I didn't think Courtney would have any trouble. It wasn't like she was *exactly* fat, but she was kind of big. She wasn't real girly, either. I wasn't even going to stop to help her till she started acting funny. Finally, I leaned out and held out my hand. We were going to be there all day if we just waited for her. She grabbed my hand like she was drowning. Then she ran and stood over by Jeanie.

"I think I just had my period," she said breathlessly to Jeanie, looking dreamily over at me.

About to walk, I stopped. I knew what those were because of my sister. That just happened, but not just because a girl got scared or touched a boy. It was a girl thing, but not like that. Courtney must have been talking about something else. I didn't get it, but I didn't want to say anything either.

"The lookout fort is up here," I said, walking around Jeanie and Courtney. Jeanie mumbled and Courtney laughed again when I walked by. I ignored them. If they were going to be like that then I just wouldn't care.

The lookout fort was a high spot, big and flat, hidden by a couple trees. You could look down through at Nicky's house. Nicky's dad was throwing toys from his yard onto his porch.

"See," I told Joy as I walked up. "We had a big piece of plywood up against the trees there so it was real secret up here, but somebody took it."

Joy walked up. There wasn't much to see since the board was gone, though.

Courtney was staring at me, not the fort. She looked back at Jeanie. Then she started laughing again.

I started thinking they weren't laughing at me. I didn't like Courtney the way I liked Joy, but she wasn't ugly or anything. Her hair was dirty blond, but afro puffy. Not nice and straight like Joy's. She was plain too. And, she was acting weird.

*****

I waited in line for lunch with my class and tried to see where Courtney was. The line was full of kids from all the way down the stairs into the lunchroom to the row of rolling lunch carts. The tables were all full of kids eating, too. Courtney wasn't anywhere. I had to try to find her. She didn't live near our block so she wouldn't just be around all the time. She was a fourth grader, not a fifth like me, so we didn't have class together. Joy said Courtney was working in the lunchroom, though.

The way Courtney acted the other day I thought maybe she had the hots for me. Like the way that one girl in *Back to the Future*. I was right, too. Joy told me. Joy got real excited when I'd asked if Courtney said anything about me. She said Courtney really liked me and asked if I really liked her. I said I guessed so.

I mean, she was okay and everything. That made Joy even more excited. She told me Courtney wanted me to ask her out.

Joy even gave me a necklace to give to Courtney. It was just a bunch of orange things on a string, but Joy said it was real expensive. The orange things were gems even though they felt like plastic. Joy said that was on purpose so it was expensive but no one would try to steal it. I didn't get why I was supposed to give it to Courtney. It wasn't like I bought it or anything. Besides, she wanted me to ask her out. It seemed funny I had to give her a present. I guessed girls liked it if they could say boys gave them stuff.

Courtney wasn't working the lunch line. The old ladies who ran things there took money and handed out the main dish. The kids that were working gave out stuff like the vegetables or fruit or milk. All they had to do was ask large or small or chocolate or white.

I sat down and ate with my class after I got my lunch. Lunch was mashed potatoes with turkey gravy all over it, yellow with little chunks of turkey. Green beans and fruit cocktail, too. Then I saw Courtney. The kids working who didn't give out stuff in the lunch line picked up trays and took trash outside. That's what Courtney was doing, picking up trays. She was too far away, though. When we walked out for recess, she was gone again. I couldn't wait around. I had to go outside with my class.

Fourth, fifth, and sixth graders had recess in the back of the school. There was blacktop with a couple of basketball hoops, but they only let us have a couple of basketballs, so not everybody could play. Around the blacktop was gravel and then the fence. There were only a couple sets of monkey bars and a jungle gym out on the gravel. All the good playground stuff was on the other side of the school, where the little kids had recess.

Usually I just wandered around the gravel or maybe sat on top of the green metal monkey bars. That day I played foursquare instead of the usual stuff because the spot for that was right over by the door to the lunchroom. The dumpster was right by the door, too, so I'd see Courtney if she took some trash out.

I kept losing. I was watching over by the dumpster and didn't pay enough attention to play the game good. Mark slammed the ball down hard in my square so it'd bounce up really high and I'd be out again. I was paying attention for once and grabbed it before it got too far. I ran back and dribbled the ball twice quick in his square. The squares were painted in white on the blacktop. "School rules," I said. "You're out." He was in the first spot. We were all going to move up one.

"No, I'm not!" he yelled. "I called no school rules. You're out!" Then I saw Courtney come out of the door, lugging a bag of trash toward the dumpster. I just walked off. "Hey," Mark cried. "Where're you going?"

"Hi," I said to Courtney as I jogged up, pulling the necklace out of my pocket.

"Hi," she said back. She looked confused at me. She was wearing a hairnet that squished down her puffy hair, and the white lunchroom kid apron. She'd just opened the dumpster and she was holding onto the bag of trash she'd been pulling along the ground. The bag was clear so I could see all the crushed milk cartons and mashed potatoes people threw away. There was milk running down one side of the bag.

I shuffled for a second. She just kept looking at me. I held out the necklace and she took it. She had the bag of trash in her other hand. "Will you go out with me?" I asked.

She looked at the necklace in her hand like she didn't know what it was or something. I shuffled around some more and waited. Joy hadn't told me I was supposed to say anything. "Okay," she said finally. She threw the trash in the dumpster.

I turned around and ran off. When I looked back, she'd already gone back inside.

*****

"I bet you can't hit the bullseye," Steven said. We were playing darts in my basement. Steven was picking at one of the old ceramic tiles coming up off the floor. They were white and black with little streaks of silver, like a chessboard.

Freddy, that jerk Steven was always hanging around with, motioned at the board with the dart, closing one eye. He was over by the wood stairs, painted gray, that led upstairs. "I bet I can." He'd already got a twenty and a ten. Steven only got twenty-five on his turn. Two tens and a five. I hadn't taken my turn yet.

"*Do it* then."

Freddy motioned with the dart a couple more times, like the first few times weren't enough. Then he threw. The dart hit the seven. Freddy looked at it for a second.

"*Told you*, penis breath," Steven sneered.

"Yeah I can," Freddy sneered back. "I just didn't feel like doing it right then, *nutsack*."

I went up to get the darts, but I waited till I was sure they were all done. Steven got me in the leg one time and we had to hide it from my parents so they didn't take the darts away. I still thought Steven saw me and threw anyway, just because he thought it'd be funny.

I held down the dartboard and pulled the darts out. The board was getting really old, like all faded black and white, and it was starting to fall apart. It'd probably break if we just grabbed the darts. The other side had thick metal wires all over it so we didn't have to be so careful. We didn't like that side, though, because the darts always bounced off. The darts were pretty old, too—thick and heavy at the brassy metal part. The backs were getting all bent and torn up. They were plastic so we'd just try to bend them back as best we could. My parents said they wouldn't buy me any more.

"I bet I still win," Freddy said.

I threw one, but only got a five. I didn't get to play much even though it was in my basement. My parents didn't like letting us play because of all the holes in the wood of the storage room wall behind the dartboard. I threw again, but only got a seven.

"I'm going to win!" Freddy smirked.

"He could still hit the bull," Steven said. I aimed really hard. I even motioned like Freddy had. A bunch of times. Then I threw.

"I won." Freddy smirked again.

The dart stuck in the white wooden wall next to the board. I looked at my hand. It had to be the ring. I had it on my pointer finger. The one next to my right thumb that I held darts with. The ring kept hitting the metal part of the dart when I tried to throw and kept messing me up. I'd worn it all the time for a week.

"What's that?" Steven pointed at the ring, seeing me look at it.

"A ring. Courtney gave it to Joy to give to me." I didn't know why, but I didn't say that. Maybe it was because I gave her the necklace.

"That's a girl's ring!"

"No it isn't," I snapped. It did look like a girl's ring, all thin with a single little red stone coming off it. Joy said it wasn't, though. "Besides," I went on, "it's expensive. Joy said it's real gold and ruby."

Steven held out his hand. "Let me see it then." I took the ring off and handed it to him. "This is junk," he said. "The rock is glued on. Real rings don't do that. This is just some crap Joy had."

Freddy laughed. "From Goodwill I bet."

"No it isn't!" I grabbed the ring back and put it on. "Courtney gave it to me. It's *real.*"

"It's junk, even if it's real," Freddy replied. "Plus, she's gross."

"No she's not!" I looked at Freddy and then at Steven. "You're both just jealous."

"I could have a girl if I wanted," Freddy coolly insisted. He sat down on the steps. Sometimes we threw darts from there to see if we still hit. That's why there were all the holes in the wall.

"Me too," Steven said as he walked up and got the darts. "I've got three girls in my class who pass me notes all the time and they're all prettier than Courtney, too."

"What are their names then," I challenged.

"Christy Michaels, Rhonda Baker, and Stephanie Silver." He smiled.

I gritted my teeth and didn't say anything. Freddy was smiling. Steven threw a dart and hit the twenty. "What do you butt-holes know anyway," I finally said.

"Plenty," they both said at the same time, sneering. They were just jealous. I bet none of those girls ever gave notes to Steven. I slipped the ring off my finger while they weren't looking. Then I stuck it into the pocket of my jeans.

## Bones Buried in the Dirt

I saw the bone sticking up out of the dirt when I was scrambling up the graveyard hill. It was on a lump that water washed down either side of when it rained. There was just a little bit sticking out. It didn't look like much, just a little something sitting there, like a rock poking out of the dirt. The hill's dirt was real packed so the little something was easy to see. I kicked the lump and a bone popped out. A bunch of dirt flew up, too, leaving a big hole.

I brushed it off to see what it was. It cleaned off pretty easy. The dirt was all dry because of the sun. The bone was all dry too. And rough. Not slick or smooth like I thought bones were. I also thought bones were white. This one was kind of goldish-brown. It was shaped like two smooshed-up tennis balls stuck together, or maybe more like two of my Duncan butterfly yo-yo's.

I ran home. Nicky's neighbor was out mowing his lawn and looked at me when I went by. "Mom, look!" I ran the bone right up to her, holding it out. She was out moving the sprinkler from one side of the yard to the other, even though the grass was already brown and dead. "I found it up on the hill!"

She looked, but didn't take it. Her nose wrinkled, which made the freckles on it jump around. "That's nice," she said, turning back to pull on the hose. The sprinkler too, turning the faded metal arms and making little bits of water pump out. "Put it back when you're done."

"But it might be from a person!" I still held it out to her, in case she wanted to look closer. "Maybe they put the fence in the wrong spot and missed some old graves!" It was important if it was a people bone. Maybe I'd get my picture in the paper.

My mom shook her head, not turning around. "It's probably just an animal, Peter. Either go and play with it or help me with this, but I have to finish. I have a shift tonight."

I walked off with the bone, like she told me. I guessed she was right. She was a nurse so she knew what people bones looked like. That's when I thought of the dig. If they weren't people bones it was okay to mess around with them. There wasn't anything I didn't know about how to do a dig because I'd gone to an archeology camp that summer. Since I'd been a fifth grader, I got to learn about what archeologists really did, not like the littler kids. The third graders just did stupid stuff like making mummy masks out of paper plates and newspaper.

My friend, Joy, from the block over was the only one around, so she was my dig team. She followed me back. "What do you think it is?" Joy asked, looking at the bone. "Maybe your mom is wrong and we'll get haunted."

"Maybe, but archeologists dig up people all the time and don't get haunted." We were over by the tree house fort. That was just a couple boards nailed to a tree branch close to the ground. People could sit there, but that was about it.

Joy squatted down by the hole. Her long light blue skirt still covered her legs so I couldn't see her panties or anything even though she was squatting. "What about the string and all the drawing stuff you said we had to do?"

I shrugged. "My mom won't let me have any string. People probably just do that so they don't forget where they found stuff. I can just remember." Joy nodded. I didn't have any little shovels or brushes either. I did have a bent pipe I could dig with, though. It was okay as long as I was careful to not break any bones.

"Maybe they're food bones," Joy suggested as I dug, "like from somebody's trash."

"Maybe." The dirt was hard on the top, but it crumbled easy, dry. There were more bones in the dirt. "They're too big for chicken, though, and they're not cut up like bones in steaks."

Most of the bones were little. Funny shaped. They didn't look anything like pictures I'd seen of skeletons. That first one was shaped right for a squirrel, but would have filled the whole fat little body. Arm bones leg bones stuck right to it. Skeletons weren't like that so it wasn't a squirrel bone. I tossed the bones in a pile over by Joy. She watched, squatting again.

"Maybe it's a dog?"

"Could be." I kept digging. Whatever they were, it seemed like it was all from the same thing. They were all the same dusty goldish-brown. Pieces of something.

"What do we do after we find all of them?"

"That's when we get to figure out what it is," I answered. "Try putting it back together. Like a jigsaw puzzle. You can even test the bones and see how old they are."

"Could we be famous?" Joy's eyes widened.

"Sure, if it's something really old. We could mount everything and label it and enter it into science fairs. I bet nobody else has stuff from a real dig."

I'd found a bunch of bones, but not enough for a full ... whatever it was. No skull or anything big like that. There were probably books I could get from the library, though, with pictures of different kinds of bones. I could figure it out from those. Real archeologists probably did that.

"It looks old," she replied, looking at the bones.

I was starting to get tired. I hadn't found anything in a while. I decided that what we'd found was all there was and stopped. Joy helped me carry the bones home. We pulled out our shirts to make baskets and carried them in that. I'd keep them in a shoebox I had until I figured out what kind of animal they were and mounted them. My mom stopped me, though, when we got to my porch.

"What's all this?" My mom blocked the way, holding open the storm door and tying her frizzy red hair back with a black ribbon. The hospital made her tie her hair back. She'd been getting ready for work when she'd seen us.

"I've got to get something to put these in," I said. Joy smiled at my mom.

"Oh, no," my mom held out her hands to stop me coming closer even though I hadn't moved. The sprinkler was still going in the yard. It was one of those little metal ones that spin around. "Those things are filthy."

"I'll wash them," I offered. My mom hated dirt. Germs. Anything. She always made me wash my hands, even when I wasn't eating. "I'll use the hose and keep them in the garage."

"No, Peter." She fixed the stiff collar of her white uniform. "They'll attract vermin."

"But I got to save them somewhere so I can find out stuff about them," I whined. I hated doing that, but I had to keep them. They wouldn't get bugs anyway. The bones weren't rotting, they were too old. There wasn't anything there for bugs to eat. My mom was just picky about stuff like that. That's why she wouldn't let me get a cat.

"They're just some old bones," she said like she knew everything.

"I can keep them at my house?" Joy suggested, smiling more at my mom.

"See?" My mom clipped on her nametag. "Joy will take them."

I ran upstairs to get the shoebox before my mom did something. She'd throw the bones out if she got the chance. Then she'd tell me she'd lost them or something, like what happened to my bottle cap collection. It wasn't fair. Archeologists got to keep lots of bones. I didn't get to do anything. I quickly ran back down.

"You got to be careful," I told Joy as I loaded up the bones. "If they break I won't be able to find out anything. And you got to bring them back when I need them."

My mom watched me, even though she had to go to work. Probably so I didn't sneak the box of bones inside when she wasn't looking.

"Don't worry," Joy said. Then she took the shoebox and walked off down the block.

\*\*\*\*\*

"We'll play 'Glory of Love' from Karate Kid," Joy told me.

"What'll I do?"

"You dress up as the knight. Then Courtney and Jeanie and me sing and dance while you pretend to ride a horse. It's a great act."

Nicky threw a wiffle ball in the air and hit it. The ball bounced off his dad's old white Buick parked by the curb. We'd been playing in his yard after dinner until it started getting dark and Joy came over. There was still plenty of light, but I stopped anyway once Joy got there. Nicky kept messing around like we were still playing.

"See? If we point to you while we dance it looks like we're singing to you."

Joy wanted to show me the moves she'd come up with for the talent show, so she was dancing to a Madonna tape playing on the boom box up on the porch. I didn't get it, since it wasn't the right music. It was Nicky's boom box, but it wasn't Nicky's tape. Joy was mainly just swaying back and forth and doing different stuff with her arms. I didn't know much about dancing, though. That was probably what dancing was supposed to look like. The whole thing seemed kind of dumb to me, but Joy was really excited, so I guess it was okay.

Joy said they were going to have matching outfits too. She said maybe they'd get strapless Hawaiian dresses and put flowers in their hair. Of course, she also said maybe they'd get fifties sweaters and poodle skirts too. She wasn't wearing any of that. She had on a black denim skirt and a red sleeveless shirt with plastic buttons up the front instead. She also had a black headband holding her long hair back out of her face.

Nicky was trying to bounce the ball on the wiffle bat. It wasn't too hard, the bat was one of those fat, red plastic ones, but his stringy brown hair kept getting in his eyes. He didn't seem real interested in Joy's dancing. Probably because he wasn't in the show.

"When a girl loves a boy," Joy sang along, "and a boy...loves...a girl." She folded her arms out in front of her and then pointed at me. "Like you and Courtney." She smiled.

I didn't smile. I'd actually just been thinking how good Joy looked in the sleeveless shirt. I crossed my arms over my chest.

"Hey," Nicky said, sounding interested all of a sudden. He was looking up at the hill to the graveyard. Nicky's house was right across the street from there. Joy and I looked. There was something up at the top, just a little bit across the alley from us, walking in the trees. It turned to look at us, but kept walking.

"That's a wolf," I said, even though I knew it couldn't be. It looked like one of those homeless people downtown, fur all raggedy and mussed up. The wolf was even slumping its shoulders while it walked. I saw its eyes when it looked at us, all yellow and weird looking. I was backing up without thinking. Wolves ate people.

"What should we do?" Nicky held up the wiffle bat, like he was going to use that if the wolf went for us. He looked silly like that because he was so skinny and little.

The wolf just kept walking along the top of the hill. He wasn't running exactly, but he was walking pretty fast. It looked like he was hurrying somewhere. Then, an animal control van came rolling slowly down the alley. We watched as the wolf and the van disappeared down toward Joy's block. The Madonna tape stopped.

Suddenly, there were people everywhere. Everyone came running out of their houses to look. I couldn't figure out who told them. Everybody ran around and talked all at once. "They were keeping it as a pet," I heard somebody say. "But they left it when they moved out. It got out and has been running around, loose." "It attacked a child yesterday," somebody else said. "It got scared off when a parent showed up."

My dad was in Nicky's yard too. He pointed at me, looking angry like I'd done something bad. "Stay here. I don't want you moving until I get back." He walked off down the alley toward where the wolf and the van had gone.

"That goes for you too, Nicky," Nicky's dad said. He'd been standing next to the wooden porch swing and looking quietly at everyone. He was bald and had a big bristly beard he was stroking.

"I'm going to make sure he didn't go to my house," Joy said and went running off. She didn't follow down the alley, though. She ran the other way around the block.

Nicky and I just stood around his yard. People started calming down and going back in their houses. My dad still hadn't come back. I worried maybe the wolf got him. Joy came running back. She was breathing fast like she'd run the whole way.

"Did he go to your house?" Nicky asked.

"No," Joy replied. "But he was going that way. He must have smelled all those bones we found. I scattered them all around the yard to confuse him."

I sagged. "What?! You threw out all the bones?"

"Yup," Joy beamed. "I bet he was so hungry he could smell them all the way in the house.

That was stupid. Wolves could smell good, but not that good. The bones were so old they probably didn't smell like anything anymore. The wolf probably wouldn't have wanted them anyway. Chewing on old bones wasn't food, but I didn't say anything. I just glared at Joy.

Later, I went to her yard and looked all around in the grass, but I couldn't find them. All I found was a broken piece or two of something. I wasn't even sure the pieces were mine. They were white, not gold. I didn't even pick them up. I'd never find out what kind of thing they were. I remembered what they looked like, but that wouldn't be enough. I couldn't find out anything anymore.

I started thinking maybe the wolf had come and got them after all. Maybe just to chew on. Except, I knew that wasn't true. The animal control people had picked him up a couple blocks past Joy's block. They had to. Wolves can't be around people anymore once they attack a kid. My dad saw them. He said they just opened up the back and stayed back and the wolf just walked inside all by himself. Maybe the wolf just wanted to get away from everybody.

# Druthers Part 2

We were all standing around in Joy's backyard. She was filling up their small wading pool so she could swim in it with her littlest sister and Courtney. Courtney was officially my girlfriend. That dork, Nicky, from over on my block came, too. Even Bobby from a couple blocks away was there.

"Look out," Joy taunted, putting her finger over the hose so it sprayed at Bobby.

"Cut it out!" He jumped back out of the way. He wore a yellow shirt with a little alligator sewn on it and nice new slacks, not a swimsuit like Joy. He was wearing penny loafers, too.

Joy laughed and went back to filling up the green plastic wading pool. It was pretty raggedy-looking, all dented in parts and torn up top like it was from Goodwill. There were little fish shapes stamped in it, where they weren't too smashed to see. Her littlest sister, Nadine, was standing in the ankle-deep water. She had a suit on, too.

"It's just water," Courtney said, kind of snotty-like. She was standing by me.

"See how *you* like it then," Nicky said as he scooped water out of the pool at her. She squealed, jumping back and blocking the water with her arms, even though she was wearing a suit. Nicky wasn't, but his clothes weren't nice so he probably didn't care. There were juice stains on them. I got out of the way, though, so I didn't get splashed.

Courtney didn't look cute in her suit the way Joy did. Joy's suit was sleek and black. She was tan and it looked good. Courtney's was kind of freaky; blue and pink and yellow with all sorts of green ruffles all over it. There was a green skirt thing to it, too, whatever that was supposed to be. It looked like it had some kind of stupid island theme or something. She was pale

too and that just made it look worse. "It's still cold," she
protested, though not as snotty as before.

Joy finished filling the wading pool and dropped the
hose. All the water was making it muddy under the grass. Nadine
plopped down in the pool and started splashing around. She was
six. It was a tiny little wading pool. They couldn't all sit down in
it at the same time, especially not Courtney.

"Who cares if the water's cold," Nicky said as he
splashed himself, somehow not washing any of the grime off.
"It's hot." It was hot. Humid, too. My parents said you weren't
supposed to swim if it wasn't eighty. It was probably a hundred
or more, though.

Courtney was looking at me. She looked away when
she saw me see her, like she was pretending to be shy. "Hey,"
Joy said, nodding at Courtney, "let's play a game."

"What kind of game?" I asked.

She kneeled down and put her hands on her legs. "A
dare game," she whispered. Courtney was looking at me again.
Nobody said anything. Joy looked around. Nadine was still
splashing in the pool. "Peter, I dare you to kiss Courtney."

"What? No way," I said. "Everybody can see us."

Courtney glared at Joy, her lips all scrunched up like an
earthworm. Then she pointed her chubby chin up and pretended
to look at a cloud. Joy jumped up and grabbed a thin blue wool
blanket wadded up by her backdoor. "Here, lean over the pool
and we'll cover you. Nadine, get out."

I thought maybe Nadine wouldn't get out. She did,
though. She hopped right out, grinning. "It looks dirty," I said.

Joy shook the blanket a bunch of times in the air.
"There, it's fine."

I didn't move toward the pool. Courtney did, though. She walked and sat down over by it. Not in it, just leaning over it with her chunky legs tucked under herself.

Everyone was looking at me.

"All right," I said finally. I sat down over by Courtney. She smirked. We both leaned over the pool and Joy threw the blanket over us. It was really shadowy under there, like my basement, even though sun still came through the blanket. Courtney's face looked puffy, gray even. I could still see her shape, sort of, but she looked like she was slapped together out of a big lump of clay. It was hotter under there, too. Like the air was thicker, or something. I tried to get close and kiss her. Get it over with. It wasn't like I couldn't find her or something. The air just seemed heavy, like it was pushing on me and I couldn't move. The blanket was scratchy and itchy, too. Air didn't move through real well.

Courtney pushed her head toward me, eyes screwed shut and her lips mashed together like squashed tomatoes. It stunk like old peoples' feet under the blanket. I kept thinking the smell was Courtney all sweaty and dirty or something. Joy probably smelled good, like cocoa butter. I thought about how Joy looked in her swimsuit. Courtney got even closer.

Suddenly, I jumped up and threw the blanket off.

"Did you do it?" Joy smiled.

"I can't breathe under there!" I flapped my arms, taking deep breaths.

Courtney stood up and stomped off to the side of the pool. She slapped hard at the dorky green ruffles on the bottom of her suit, like they'd somehow gotten mashed down and she was trying to straighten them. Joy started chewing on her lip.

"What now?" Nicky looked at Joy.

Joy looked like she was thinking. "Okay," she said, "I dare Bobby to kiss me."

Bobby's eyes opened wide and then went back again. He shrugged and sat down Indian-style by the pool. He didn't seem real excited, though. He didn't even bother to lean over. I bet she just wanted to kiss him because he was dressed all preppy, like he was a stock broker or something. I didn't like Bobby very much right then, but I held the blanket over them. A few seconds later, Joy lifted it. She smiled and they both stood up.

"Nothing to it," Bobby said. I didn't look at Courtney. She was probably looking at me again.

Nicky ran over by the pool. "It's my turn now. Who do I get to kiss?"

Joy looked around, pretending to think. "How about Nadine?" Nadine made a kissy face and giggled.

"No way," Nicky yelled. "That's not fair. She's little."

"Oh well," Joy shrugged. "Guess you don't get to kiss anybody." Nicky frowned and kicked the pool. A little water splashed out. He didn't say anything. Nadine just giggled again.

"It's your turn then, Peter." Joy smirked at Courtney. "Me and Bobby could breathe."

I slowly marched to the pool. Courtney plodded over, too.

"Peter!" It was my sister. She'd walked up Joy's driveway when we weren't looking. She had long, nasty brown hair that was all wavy and stuff. Her bangs rolled up in one of those dumb shredded wheat puff things, like she'd been messing with hairspray again even though she wasn't going anywhere. "Mom and Dad say you've got to come home. It's time for lunch."

I shrugged and jogged quick over to her. "Bye," they all said as I left.

I followed my sister out of the backyard. We turned when we got to the street to go to our block. "Well," she said, all smug, "it's good I came when I did, isn't it? They were going to make you kiss that girl."

"So? She's my girlfriend."

Her bossy mouth hung open. That shut her up. She thought she was so smart because she was in junior high. I had a girlfriend already, though, and she'd never gone out with anyone. She didn't say anything the rest of the way home.

*****

Steven pedaled his black BMX bike really hard. His hair would have blown around if he hadn't just gotten it butched short again. It made his head look big. Then he slammed the brakes. His back tire skidded and left a long black mark. "Ha! *Cool*," he said.

Joy and her stupid little sister, Jeanie, were coloring with chalk on the sidewalk down by Nicky's house. It was Nicky's chalk that he'd left outside, not theirs. I didn't know what they were drawing because I was riding bikes in the street with Steven.

Whipping my handlebars to the left, I swung in a circle. Then I pedaled to catch up with Steven. Steven turned in his driveway and I followed. We rode to the other end of the block on the sidewalk. Then we turned out another driveway onto the street again just before the intersection. We kept turning until we were pointing down toward Joy.

I started thinking, looking at Joy. She wasn't paying attention to us. She was just coloring with the chalk, bits of her long hair falling in front of her face like a curtain.

"Ready, Agent Peter?"

"Huh?" I snapped out of it.

"I *said*, are you *ready*?" Steven asked again.

I was by the Peterson's new Oldsmobile. Their house was next door to mine.

"Ready," I said, scooting my bike in front. It wasn't an Oldsmobile anymore. It was a Russian spy car. Just like *Spies Like Us*. They knew I had microfilm that could ruin their plans and they were trying to stop me. I started riding away.

Steven started pedaling, too, along next to me, but he wasn't being chased. He didn't have the microfilm this time.

"Oh no! They released the heat seeking missiles. Better go faster!"

I rode faster. The missiles were right behind me. If I didn't go fast enough, they'd get me. I couldn't just ride away. The missiles would follow. Steven pedaled faster, too. The missiles were by where he was. They followed me along the crack in the pavement.

"They're gaining," Steven yelled. "Better try to go faster!"

I rode even harder. He did, too. I had to go fast enough, but not too fast. If I got too far ahead, then the trick wouldn't work and the missiles would still get me. I couldn't just ride faster than them forever. I had to get it just right.

"They're right on your tail!"

I swerved off just before the asphalt patch the city fixed the street with. That was really a wall. The missiles were too close. Before they could turn, they already hit the wall and exploded.

"Boom!" Steven threw up his arms. I didn't even have to turn to see him do it. We always did that. It was part of the game.

I coasted along, having beaten the Russians once more. Steven was still cheering. I looked up and saw Joy. Quickly, I started pedaling. Steven pedaled, too, but he hung back a bit. I got up on the sidewalk and rode fast toward Joy. I stopped right before the spot where Joy and Jeanie were drawing. Joy peeked up at me.

"I don't want Courtney to be my girlfriend anymore," I said. "I want to go out with you."

Joy stared, eyes all big. She smoothed her hair out of her face, but didn't talk. She blinked. Jeanie glared, like she was really mad. Joy was still holding a white piece of chalk. She'd been drawing a picture of a big green house with little red chalk trees in the yard. Palm trees.

I turned and hit the pedals, launching off the curb into the street. Steven sat on his bike a little way away, watching. He joined me as I passed, looking at me and then at Joy.

"Peter!" My dad called out my front door. "The dishwasher is done! Better empty it if you want your allowance!"

Joy walked right out in front of me just as I was about to turn into my driveway. I stopped. "Peter? Do you promise you won't do to me what you did to Courtney?"

"Sure."

"Okay then." She turned and walked back down the block. Jeanie stared, grinding a piece of chalk into the ground. Steven watched and turned more circles. I rode right up my driveway hill and didn't even have to stop once like I usually did.

*****

"Just pull yourself up," Steven told Freddy.

Steven and me were sitting on my swing set. We'd swung from one of the monkey bars until we caught a foot over and pulled ourselves up. There wasn't room for Freddy to do that with me and Steven up there. Instead, Freddy jumped up as high as he could off the step and grabbed onto the top. Then he just wriggled up and sat down. Me and Steven shifted over for him.

My swing set was one of those tan four-post ones with dark brown and orange stripes running all over it. There were monkey bars going down the middle and swings and a trapeze coming off the sides. It used to wiggle too much, but it was okay once my dad put cement around the posts. I played on it a lot, when I was little.

Then I saw Joy walk up my driveway. She wore a long orange floppy skirt and a jean jacket with shiny things all over it. Buttoned all up the front with the sleeves cuffed at her elbows. Her long brown hair was pushed back out of her face by a black plastic headband. She stopped by my swing set, holding a hand over her eyes to block the sun so she could see us.

"Hi," I said, eagerly leaning over the monkey bars to get closer. Steven and Freddy groaned. They didn't like Joy. She just looked at them.

"I can't be your girlfriend," she told me. "My mom said."

"What?" I sat up too fast and had to catch myself so I didn't slip. I thought Steven and Freddy would laugh, but they stayed quiet. I wasn't smiling anymore. "Why?"

"Jeanie tattled and my mom got mad. My dad, too. They didn't like it that you put Nadine's Barbie in the trash."

"So? I gave it back when she started crying." It wasn't a big deal. I just did it to mess with her. It'd only been a couple days since Joy said she'd go out with me.

"They still said no." She messed with her hair, like it might not be straight even though it was back in a headband.

"But … we could still go out," I suggested. Joy crossed one leg behind the other, standing there kind of like a stork. Freddy whispered something to Steven. "And just not tell anyone."

She frowned. "No, I don't want to get in trouble. Jeanie will find out. Somebody'll tell." She looked at Steven and Freddy again.

I looked away. All we had to do was not tell anybody. I could do that. She could too. She just didn't want to. It was like she didn't even want to go out. I bet that was it. She just didn't want to say it and get everybody mad at her.

Forget that.

I wasn't that dumb.

"So," I snapped, "if we're not going out why don't you go home? You don't have to hang out here anymore."

"I need to tell Freddy something," she snapped back, crossing her arms. "Something private about Courtney." She waited like she thought he'd get down and go with her. He didn't. Then she just said, "Courtney's mom said not to say stuff about Steven on their answering machine anymore. If you act like that then she can't go out with either of you."

Courtney started going out with both of them when I dumped her. It wasn't fair. They both had girlfriends and I didn't have any. Courtney probably just did it to get me back.

Steven smacked Freddy on the arm. "What did you say about me?"

"He said that you didn't really like her. He said that she should break up with you because you only wanted her to make out with you," Joy tattled.

"No I didn't!"

Steven pushed Freddy, or he tried to. It was hard to push somebody on top of a swing set. "Why'd you do that?"

"I *didn't*," Freddy protested. "Anyway, it's true. You said you were going to get her to go up in the trees on the hill and get naked. You *said that*!"

They rolled around, trying to push each other off. They looked like those wrestlers on TV. Nobody probably wrestled on top of monkey bars, though. I scooted all the way down to the other end. I didn't want to fall just because they were being stupid.

"She wouldn't do that stuff with you, anyway," Freddy yelled. "She likes *me* better."

"She would so," Steven screamed back. "I bet you she'd come over right now and do it. She just felt sorry for you. That's the only reason she went out with you in the first place."

I thought one of them would fall, but they weren't moving each other much. They just kept yelling and pushing. I checked to see if Joy was laughing, if this was why she'd told. She wasn't even watching them, though. She stared off at something, almost sad. I looked and saw the wilted little tree over by my driveway, one of the ones that kept popping from the helicopters off the really big tree in the center of the yard.

Maybe that's what she was looking at. It didn't do any good if she felt bad for it. My dad said he was just going to cut it down anyway.

# Playing War

My friend Steven pulled the trigger on his plastic machine gun; it was long and mostly black with brown only where wood was supposed to be. The gun sounded "*tat-tat-tat-tat.*"

He pointed it at Mr. Pang's bramble bush. We were in Mr. Pang's front yard.

"I'm John Rambo," he said. "Okay, Peter?"

I looked over at Steven lying in the dirt next to me. "Why do you get to be Rambo?"

"Because it was my idea to play." He pulled the trigger again, but slow. Lazy. "*Da-thhat-da-da-thhhat-thhat-that,*" the gun wheezed. It made sounds as often as the trigger pulled, but it had to be fast to sound right.

"Who do I get to be then?" I asked. I cocked my rifle and shot at the bush, too. It made a popping noise. The rifle was metal and heavy. The butt was even real wood. It only fired once at a time, though, and didn't sound real.

"You can be the colonel," Steven offered, squinting one eye to aim.

"Who's that?" I didn't remember anything about a colonel. I'd never seen Rambo. My dad said he had to be there if I watched grown up movies, but he couldn't watch anything about the war anymore. He'd get all shaky and stuff when he tried, like he was really cold.

"He's Rambo's commander! He gets to give Rambo missions and stuff. He wears a beret and tells Rambo what to do. Rambo's better, but the Colonel's still pretty cool."

We were hiding in Mr. Pang's flowers that grew in a row along the front of the house. They were those tall kind of flowers with the big orange bells and long, stiff stems growing out of a big mess of leafy stuff. When flowers fell off, the stems dried out like weak forked sticks. They pulled right out when tugged on and were good for sword fights, even if they broke easy. My dad still didn't want me playing with sticks, but these weren't sticks. All that leafy stuff hid us pretty good. Not like the bramble bush in the middle of the yard. It was big and all, but we could see right through it. We got stuck when we tried to go in, too. The flowers were better.

Mr. Pang's yard was a good spot to play guns. With the flowers and bush it was like a jungle, even if it was the middle of our block *and* daytime. Mr. Pang didn't care. He was never home, anyway. It was better than my yard or Steven's.

"So, what orders am I supposed to give you?" I asked. I cocked my rifle.

"Pretend we're talking on walkie-talkies," he said. "We're both in the jungle, but I'm in deeper." Then he told me what orders to give him.

"Rambo," I said, talking into my hand. "There's a POW camp near you."

"Roger that." Steven held his hand up to the side of his head and talked into it.

"It's too heavily guarded for just one soldier, so wait and I'll bring reinforcements."

"*No can do*, colonel." Steven scrunched down on his stomach and pointed the machine gun ahead. "Those POWs can't wait—I'm going in." He crawled out from behind the flowers. Then he turned and squirmed across the yard towards the bramble bush.

"What? I just gave you an order. You're supposed to wait."

"John Rambo doesn't listen to orders," Steven insisted, still crawling.

I watched him go. It wasn't any fun if he wouldn't listen. That was stupid. He'd do all the fun stuff. He always did things like that.

"*Rambo! Come in,*" I yelled. Steven pretended to throw the walkie-talkie away. Then he kept crawling, staring ahead like he couldn't see me. I got down and crawled after him. The colonel probably never went into the jungle, but I did. It was better than doing nothing.

"*Ah! Ambush,*" Steven said and plunked the machine gun back off at the flowers. He ducked every once in a while even though he was already on the ground, like the ambush shot back. I fired my rifle a couple times. We weren't supposed to be in the same place, but I just pretended I'd found my own ambush. Just a couple guys, though. I only had the rifle, not a machine gun, like Steven's.

"*There's too many!*" he cried. "I'll have to use a grenade." He grabbed a chunk of cement and pretended to pull something off it. Then he threw. "*Bkhshh,*" he shouted, shielding himself with his arms, as the chunk bounced a couple times on the ground.

"Ha! What a bunch of babies," that butthole PJ laughed and pointed. Steven and me looked up. He was standing on the sidewalk with his friend Jeff and some other guy.

They hadn't come around from their block for forever, ever since we won the war. I'd never seen the other guy before at all. He looked like Jeff, but shorter and not so skinny—almost puffy. Especially his cheeks, like a squirrel eating nuts. He still wasn't as short and pudgy as PJ, though.

"They're playing soldiers!" PJ twisted his short little neck toward Jeff and the other guy. "They must still be second graders!"

"*No.* I'm in *fifth!*" I shouted, but I didn't say anything about Steven. He got held back and was in fourth grade because of reading. I didn't know what grade PJ and Jeff were, but I bet it wasn't sixth. They went to that Catholic school where everybody thought they were so great.

"You play baby games," he sneered, wrinkling his nose. "I didn't think they let babies in the fifth grade." Jeff and the other guy laughed, probably pretending they thought it was funny, even though it wasn't.

I gritted my teeth. I wanted to make them stop. Steven didn't even do anything.

"No, we're *not*! Guns aren't for babies," I yelled.

PJ stepped up, like he was getting ready to punch somebody. Jeff and the other guy watched us and PJ, like they were waiting for something to start. "I say they are. What're you going to do? Shoot me with your toy, *baby*?" I swallowed. "That's what I thought." He turned and started strutting away. "Leave the babies to their baby games."

I looked over at Steven. He grinned. "Give them the finger. Then run for my porch." I nodded. Then Steven jumped up to his feet and I did the same. "Hey, PJ," he yelled.

They turned back and we did it. Middle fingers flying, waving with both hands. Steven bugged out his eyes with his head tilted and stuck out his tongue, so I did that, too.

"Get those dorks!" PJ yelled and charged at us on his stubby legs. We ran. They came up the yard, but we ran the other way around the bramble bush and out into the street. Steven ran straight for his porch, but I went right so he was nearer them than me. If they caught us they'd get him first. They ran right past him, though, and went for me.

The three of them caught me in Steven's neighbor's yard. Jeff and the other guy grabbed my arms and PJ punched me in the stomach. Steven didn't stop to look. He just left me behind and kept running. I didn't even see him look back once he was safe on his porch.

I probably wouldn't have either, but he was supposed to be Rambo.

"Don't let him get away," PJ ordered. Jeff and the other guy grimaced and grabbed harder like PJ told them to. It hurt my shoulders the way they pulled my arms directions they didn't go. Then PJ punched me in the stomach again.

I thought I was going to throw up.

"So, baby plays soldiers 'cause he's *tough*? How tough are you *now*?"

I couldn't breathe enough to answer. He punched me again anyway. "Crap," PJ said, stopping.

I managed to look up and saw a car driving by. Maybe PJ worried it'd see and he'd get in trouble. It wasn't anybody from our block, though. It was just that beat up, black car from over on Joy's street, the one that looked like it was supposed to be a truck. The back was all full of old wood and bricks. It parked at that abandoned-looking house next door to Joy, the one where that kid my sister's age that actually got expelled was supposed to live.

"What do we do?" Jeff looked wide-eyed at PJ, mouth hanging open. PJ stared at the car, but it didn't stop. Jeff and the other guy weren't paying attention to me so I broke away. I was already running before they even noticed.

*Dummies.*

"*Catch him!*" PJ screeched as I ran for Steven's porch.

Even with the head start, they were still right behind me. I leapt up over the stairs and threw myself at the door. Steven wasn't anywhere to be seen. He must have hidden inside. PJ, Jeff, and the other guy didn't come up onto Steven's porch, but they didn't leave right away either. They stood out in the yard, glaring. PJ rubbed his stupid, blond shaved head, like he was thinking. Jeff pulled up his long shorts showing his bony

knees. His shorts were probably loose because he was too skinny
for them. I worried PJ and them would wait until I came out and
get me. I couldn't stay at Steven's forever, even if I went inside.

After a while, though, they slunk off. PJ gave me a
nasty look, his face all twisted up, as he left.

*****

"Come on! Stop dragging!" My dad stomped across the
street. He didn't even stop to look for cars. He was tense,
pumping his fists.

The whole time, he kept grinding his teeth.

I just trailed behind. When he noticed, he yelled at me
to hurry, so I ran up close. When he wasn't paying attention,
though, I drifted back again.

"Get moving," he yelled again, storming down towards
PJ's block. "I'm talking to this little prick for *you*, not my health."

I'd told my dad. I'd hoped he'd yell at PJ, maybe scare
him into leaving me alone. He didn't, though. Instead he said we
were going to PJ's house to talk to his dad. I had to go along.

"This is bullshit," my dad growled as we rounded the
corner. "He lets his kid run wild, and then *I* have to deal with it."
My dad shook his head. "That just isn't going to fly. He's going
to keep his in line."

I didn't say anything. I didn't think he wanted me to.
He never stopped long enough. Didn't turn around to look at
me, either. I just kept following.

"Which house does this brat live in?" he demanded. I
jumped. Then I pointed and my dad charged up PJ's sidewalk.
There was a beat-up white van in PJ's driveway. *Senderson
Plumbing* was written in big red letters on the side. The hood was

open and a big fat guy in blue overalls was messing around in there. He looked up, but he didn't take his hands off what he was doing.

"Yeah?" He grunted. "Help you?"

"You PJ's father?" My dad crossed his arms over his chest. He squeezed his fists a couple times, like that one time when the policeman kept writing out a ticket, even though my dad came to put money in the meter.

"Yep, that's me." He wiped his forehead with his arms, keeping his greasy hands away from his face. Then wiped some of the grease off with an even greasier rag tucked into the bumper. "What can I do for you?"

PJ's dad was bigger than my dad. Fatter, but just bigger too. PJ's dad had a potbelly, like this bear we saw when my parents took me to Yellowstone. My dad clenched his teeth for a second. "Your son beat up on my son. Got a couple friends to hold him down and then worked him over."

PJ's dad's narrowed his eyes angrily at my dad. "Oh he did, did he?"

My dad flexed. "Thought I'd come and see what we could do about it."

"Well..." PJ's dad said, chewing on something. He turned toward the house. "*PJ! Get your butt out here!*"

"*Coming,*" PJ called from inside the house. I heard him through a screen door by the van.

"I said *now!*" PJ came running out. He stopped when he saw my dad and me. The screen door slammed behind him. His dad stood up. "You been fighting? You gang up on this kid?"

"It wasn't like that," PJ whined. "He flipped us–" PJ's dad whacked him one quick on the back of the head. Not hard, but quick. He didn't seem to be worried about greasy hands anymore.

"I don't care what he did," his dad said, pointing his finger in PJ's face. His dad was angry, but PJ didn't cringe like he was worried about getting hit again. "I care about what *you* did. You know better than this."

PJ put his hands in his pockets. He looked at his feet and drooped his shoulders. He was still paying attention, though. "That's what I thought," his dad went on. "Now, am I going to hear about this again?"

"No, sir."

"Good. Now get back in the house. This ain't a tea party and you ain't wearing a dress."

PJ didn't look at us. My dad and I watched him slink off, though.

The screen door slammed again and I looked at my dad. He was still looking at the door. He wasn't tense anymore. His hooked his thumbs in his pockets. "Hey," my dad said finally, "sorry to nag you about your kid. You know how it is. I just thought we'd nip this in the bud."

PJ's dad held up his hands. "No no no. I would have done the same thing. If my kid's raising hell, I want to know about it. I mind my kid." He pointed a thumb back at his house. "But you can't know that until you come and talk to me."

"Sure. This kid is no angel either, but–"

"Hey," PJ's dad interrupted. "No kid is."

"I hear you," my dad agreed.

"Anyway, not to brush you off or anything, but I got to get this heap running or I'm not getting to work in the morning."

"No problem," my dad replied, holding out his hand. "Stan."

"Hank. Nice to meet you," he grabbed my dad's hand. They both gave a good shake.

*****

"All you got to do is climb up, hang there on that branch," Steven pointed. "Thirty seconds, and then drop. It's easy." We were up on the graveyard hill. Me, Steven, and dipwad Freddy.

I looked up at the tree. It was a big old dead one. The branch was high, higher than the graveyard fence. It leaned out over the alley so the drop wasn't that far, but I'd still fall onto the hill and not flat ground.

"If it's so easy," I replied, "then why doesn't *Freddy* do it?" Freddy stood at the top of the hill by the fence with Steven and me. He looked up at the tree and shrugged like it was no big deal. Like it was so easy for him that he didn't even need to bother.

"*Because.* He did it already when you weren't around. So he's an officer in the club and you're only a private. If you don't do it then you'll have to do what he says."

I bet Freddy never did.

I bet he didn't want to and Steven didn't make him and they just lied so I had to. "Did you do it?"

"It's my club, so I'm already an officer. I don't have to do anything."

I looked at the tree again. "But if I do it, then I'm an officer and won't have to do what Freddy says?"

"Right. Neither of you can order the other one around. You'll just have to do what I say."

Freddy kicked a rock with the side of his foot like it was a soccer ball. He thought he was so good at soccer, like anyone cared about that. "Let's just go do something else," he said. "This is boring if he's not going to do it."

"I'm going to!" I yelled, grabbing a hold of the tree. "Just give me a minute!" The tree bark was really thick and bumpy. I got my hands and toes into spots between the bumps and pulled, shimmying up the tree. It was scratchy, though, and my arms got all scraped as I climbed.

"You got to hang on for thirty full seconds," Steven called up, "or it doesn't count."

"Yeah," Freddy butted in, smirking like a dork. "And we'll count so you don't cheat."

"*Fine*. I don't care," I snapped back, climbing toward the branch. He probably just thought I couldn't do it like he said' he could.

This was dumb. We were the only ones in the club.

Steven wouldn't let Nicky or Joy in, even just so we'd have privates to order around. We were all going to be officers and there wasn't going to be anybody to be in charge of.

Still, I couldn't let Freddy be higher than me.

"See? I told you it was easy," Steven insisted. He held his hand over his eyes as he looked up at me, like he was keeping the sun out even though it wasn't shining on him. "You're already at the branch. Now just hang from it."

"I'm going to." I tried to get onto the branch without looking down. I just grabbed it and swung out. The bark scraped me hard and I almost let go. "Start counting! You got to start as soon as I'm hanging."

"One one-thousand. Two one-thousand..." Freddy counted real slow, on purpose. Stephen laughed.

"Hey! That's not fair. Count right." My arms were starting to hurt. I'd let go too soon if he kept counting like that.

"We got to count real seconds," Steven explained. He was still kind of laughing. "It won't count if they're not real ones."

"Fine!" I yelled, my arms burning. "Just keep counting!" I felt sure I had to have been hanging there more than thirty seconds by then, counting all the time Freddy wasn't counting.

I was going to be there forever.

"Three one-thousand. Four one-thousand..." Freddy continued even slower now, probably just to show me I wasn't the boss of him.

I stopped listening. It was harder to hang on while listening and thinking how far off thirty was.

My arms felt numb.

"*Thirty* one-thousand..." he finally said.

I made sure he got done before I let go. He'd try to say I didn't do it the full time if he wasn't all the way done saying the words. Freddy was like that. I looked down when I dropped and my arms grabbed at the branch again. It was too late, though, and I started running when I hit the ground. The dirt was soft and my shoes stuck in a little. I ran down the slope to the edge of the alley.

PJ and Jeff were standing there.

"We want to talk to you dweebs," PJ said. His cheeks and lips twitched and wrinkled when he said it, like he was trying to talk all tough. He was in front, stubby plump arms folded across his chest. Jeff was behind him. His arms were crossed, too. He looked like he was just trying to copycat PJ.

Steven and Freddy came down the hill and stood next to me. We all looked at PJ and Jeff, making sure they weren't up to something.

"We want to settle this," PJ continued, sticking out his chin. "and show you guys who's boss."

"*Yeah?*" Steven stepped forward. "How so?"

"My dad said we can't fight," PJ glared at me, "so we do something that's not fighting–we have a *war*. Your guys against our guys. Right before school starts up again. Whoever wins, *wins*. No parents, no running and tattling to your dads if you lose," he snarled at me. "*Deal?*"

I didn't answer. We didn't have to win, didn't have to show him *anything*. His dad wouldn't let him start trouble, so we didn't have to have a stupid war. Especially one with stupid rules.

"*Deal,*" Steven said.

"*What?*" I gaped at him.

"I said *deal.*" He shot me a look, then went back to staring down PJ. "We do it on the graveyard hill. And *we'll* win. We won last time."

PJ's eyes got big, surprised. He laughed. "*What?* You didn't win *that!* We just took off after we smacked him in the head with that bottle in case you babies told on us. Anyway, we'll win this one–we'll get my big brother."

"*Fine.* Get your brother. I don't care." Steven sneered.

"Good." PJ sneered crazily back, like he was making fun of Steven.

PJ and Jeff didn't move after that, but nobody said anything. Then they strutted off down the alley towards their block. They turned back a few times, acting like they were looking at stuff other than us.

"Why'd you say yes?" I shouted at Steven once they were gone. "His brother's in *high school!* They're going to cream us!"

Freddy watched Steven. His face was pinched, like he didn't like it much either. He didn't say it, though, probably to make it seem like he didn't care either way, just so he looked braver than me.

Steven stepped back. "*Hey*, I'm the leader! If I say we're going to have wars, we're going to have wars. You're my officers, so you do what I say," he said to us, though he only poked me in the chest. "*Anyway*, don't worry. He can bring his stupid brother. We'll ambush them."

"*How?*" Freddy finally piped up.

"We make monkey bridges out of rope in the trees and stuff," Steven said. "My scout book shows how to make them. We can get all that stuff at Canfield's and make all sorts of secret trails through the trees that they don't know about. Then we can sneak around in the dark and grab them. Tie them with electric tape. Canfield's has army face paint, too. We'll be invisible." Steven's eyes got all wild looking.

"You really think so?" I asked, unsure.

"*Yeah!*" He started talking real fast, not even looking at us anymore. "We can make traps, too. We got lots of time, too. School doesn't start for *months*."

"Like pit traps?" I said. My parents didn't let me go out after dark, but maybe they'd let us have a sleepover on our porch. We could sneak out after they went to bed.

"*Perfect!* We can put a sheet over the foxhole fort and cover it with leaves and stuff. They'll fall in and we can get them!"

"My dad's got mosquito netting in our garage," Freddy bragged, "for, like, when we go camping. That'd work better than a dumb old sheet."

"Yeah," Steven responded. "*See?* This is going to be *great!*"

I just looked at Steven. "All right...I guess it'd be pretty neat, if had all that stuff..."

\*\*\*\*\*

"How's it going out there?" the DJ's voice broke in over the boom box sitting on my porch. "That was Whitney Houston with 'I Wanna Dance with Somebody.' *But now*, let's send out another number for everyone playing at home. B-three, that's *B-three.*"

I snatched up my bingo tickets. They were all different colors. Some were red. Some were green, or yellow, or purple. I had them spread out on our old couch so I could see them all at once. I checked, but only one ticket had that number. I *x'd* it with my marker, then I checked them all again to make double sure.

"We've got a block of Richard Marx up next," the DJ went on, "but remember to keep listening for the next number we call. We're going to make someone a winner!"

I sat back on the couch with nothing to do but wait. The station only played girl songs, but I had to have it on to be able to win.

I looked out my porch windows and tried not to listen. The song was dumb. Looking was boring, too, though. It was late, but still light outside. Summer was almost over, but it hadn't started getting dark early yet.

Still, it was too late to go out. At least since school hadn't started I wouldn't have to go to bed right away.

"Did we win yet?" Joy asked eagerly, popping open the porch door. She was wearing a long jean skirt, past her knees, and a too-big t-shirt with *Esprit* written on it, whatever that was. Her hair was tied back in a ponytail with a thick red ribbon bow.

"Nah...not yet."

She frowned and let the porch door close behind her. "Hey." She smiled again. "There was a Brodkeys catalog in the paper. We should figure out what to pick."

"That's easy. We just pick whatever costs the most. Then we sell it."

"But what if it's something ugly? Like a really ugly pair of shoes," Joy argued.

"Doesn't matter if we're just gonna sell it. Whatever costs the most is worth the most. Who cares if it's ugly?"

Suddenly I saw Steven and Freddy staring at me and Joy through the porch door. I didn't even see them walk up. Joy looked startled. I jumped up and opened the door. "Hi," I said. "What're you guys doing?"

Steven looked at Joy. She shrunk back and slid around him in the doorway, not looking at him. Then she hurried off.

After she was gone, Steven said, "It's time. Come on."

"*Huh?*"

"The *war*. We got to go have it."

"*Now?*" I thought it was still a long ways off. I tried to remember...

"Yeah. They're ready." He nodded behind him.

I looked.

PJ and Jeff were down at the end of my sidewalk. They both had big red wiffle bats. "But...we're not–we don't have any of the *stuff*." We never made any traps or anything. The whole point was to get PJ and Jeff, but we didn't have anything to get them with. I'd forgotten about it. We didn't even have electric tape.

"I know." Steven shrugged, like it sucked, but was also no big deal.

I looked at PJ and Jeff again. They were swinging the wiffle bats, pretending to hit people. Then I looked back at Steven and Freddy. They didn't even seem worried. It didn't make any sense. I was worried. PJ and Jeff were totally going to get us.

Then I had a funny thought: Steven and Freddy wouldn't have to worry if PJ and Jeff would only get *me*. Steven and Freddy could stick together. It was like how I was the only one who had to pass the test to be an officer all over again. Joy wouldn't do that, but they would. Steven and Freddy were even sneaking peaks at each other, like they had a secret.

I tried to think of something fast.

"I can't." I said. "I got to listen for this contest. Me and Joy could win diamonds or emeralds or something."

Freddy kicked the thin black metal rail on my steps. It clanged. Steven glared, but only for a second, like Freddy would give the secret away if I could tell he actually cared. Now I was sure of it. They were up to something. "You can at least come out long enough for the war," Steven argued.

"No I can't. I'll miss the numbers. If you win, you get to pick out anything at Brodkey's."

"That's stupid," Freddy muttered. "My dad gets my mom junk from there all the time. It isn't that great."

"Yeah," Steven agreed. "It's not like you'll win, anyway."

"I could too! I got three in a row already on my purple card. I just need a couple more."

"You're not going to win. You'll just sit here and we'll be doing the war without you."

They weren't buying it. I had to think of something better.

Anything.

"I can't go out anyway," I said quick. "My dad said I had to come in soon. He won't let me go up on the hill this late."

Steven and Freddy stood, frowning. Steven looked at the door to the house behind me, like he didn't believe me, but he didn't do anything else. I stood there, too. "Forget him," Freddy spat on my steps. "He isn't worth anything. Chickens just hold you back."

"*I'm not a chicken*! My dad said I had to come in."

"Whatever," Steven sneered. "Thanks for nothing."

They turned and walked back down the steps. I closed the door and sat down on the couch. I wasn't going to be a sucker. Anyway, they couldn't stay mad. I couldn't go if my dad wouldn't let me.

Steven and Freddy walked up to PJ and Jeff. They all jabbered at each other, waving their hands a lot and looking over at me. Then they all walked off. Steven and Freddy walked toward Steven's house. PJ and Jeff walked off back toward their block.

I checked my tickets again.

# Stranger

I was waiting in my room. It was quiet. I sat on my bed and stared down at my lime-green shag carpet. My little blue plastic TV–the one with a handle like a lunchbox–was on my desk. I thought about turning it on, but it only got local channels, and there wouldn't be anything on but the news. Besides, I was supposed to wait for my dad to come in.

My bedroom door swung open–hiding the Mr. T poster with all the spit wads on it–and my dad walked in. He slowly shut my door.

Closed.

Then he walked over. At first I thought he was going to sit next to me, but then he seemed to think about it, pulling out the metal folding chair at my desk and sitting there instead. I didn't know why my dad wanted to talk to me right after school. The school year had just started. I didn't think I could be in trouble *this* soon.

"Peter," he said. Then he stopped. He looked tired. "Peter," he said again, "what have you heard about Arthur Gowen?"

I blinked and tried to think. I couldn't remember who Arthur Gowen was.

"The boy that lives behind Steven's," he continued when I didn't say anything. "His house is the one that has dark brown stucco falling off. Next door to your little friend, Joy."

"Oh." That was the house where that ugly old black car that looked like it was part truck always parked. "He's the kid that got expelled," I said.

My dad ran his fingers through his mustache, cupping his hand over his chin. He'd been shaving his beard for a while, but he still let his hair and mustache go all shaggy. "That's him." He paused. "But that's not what I meant. Have you heard anything recently?" He was talking weird, all proper and stuff.

I shook my head and my bed creaked–it was really old. Not the mattress, but the bed itself. It was dark and metal, painted with some sort of black metal paint, and the head part had these faded dark wispy flowers on it. It'd been mine longer than I could remember. I didn't even know where it came from.

My dad looked down at his leather slippers and hunched his shoulders. "Arthur has been arrested."

I tried to remember what Arthur looked like. I could only remember seeing him that time playing in Steven's backyard way back. He kept doing this weird thing where he'd come out looking for his crazy brother. He said he'd escaped from the attic where they kept him locked up. Then he ran inside and changed his clothes and came outside with a cut-up t-shirt wrapped around his head, pretending to be the crazy brother.

Me and Steven didn't fall for it and we told him.

"I wanted you to hear about it from me," my dad said. He cleared his throat and tugged at the neck of his shirt. It was his black Huskers one. "Arthur has been taking his father's car and driving around."

"Driving around where?" I asked.

"He tried to get other boys–younger ones–to go with him." My dad went on like I hadn't said anything. "Apparently a couple of them did. Arthur parked behind someone's garage and made them...*do* things."

I swallowed.

My dad looked up at me. "*Sexual* things." Then he looked away, over at my brown curtains with the tan jungle scenes and no animals.

My stomach hurt. I thought about training.

"One of the boys had to go to the hospital. The police were called. Arthur won't be able to hurt anyone anymore. He's going to jail for a long time. That's what you have to do to molesters: lock them away."

My mouth tasted like when I threw up when I got stomach flu. Steven and me just trained for when we got girls. Nicky too. We didn't do that sick stuff. I wasn't one of those. They were worse than anything, worse than people who killed people. It was Steven's idea anyway. I couldn't go to jail for that. But Nicky...what if he told somebody? What if he said it was my idea? They might put me in jail and tell everyone I was one of those.

My dad put his hands together, almost like he was praying. "Peter," he said again. His voice cracked a little when he said it.

I waited. I tried to swallow again, but it felt like I couldn't. Maybe he knew already. Maybe Nicky'd told.

"Did–" He stopped again. "Did Arthur ever try to get *you* to do anything? Anything that made you feel uncomfortable?" His head was down, but his eyes were looking up at me. He looked scared.

"*No!*"

"You can tell me, Peter," my dad pleaded. "You have to know you can talk to me. If something like that happens, it isn't your fault."

"He never did anything, *honest!*"

My dad took a deep breath and exhaled loud. "*Good*," he finally said.

I tried not to look at him, but he was looking at me. I just wanted him to stop. I already told him nothing happened. It made me keep thinking of training. My head wouldn't stop twitching, like I couldn't get my neck to sit right.

"You know what to do if anybody ever tries to do anything like that to you, right?"

"*Yes,*" I said quickly.

"Run and tell an adult," he said. "Tell me, right away. Don't do anything that makes you feel funny. That's how you know. If it makes you feel funny, then it's bad. Right?"

"*Right.*"

He sighed again and stood up. Then he walked over and hugged me. Hard, hard enough to hurt a little. Like he was trying to keep me from running off. I went limp, waiting for him to let me loose.

"All right, then," he said when he finally let me go. He stood up real straight and backed up a step. Hooked his thumbs in his pockets and took another deep breath.

I was still sitting on the bed. I hadn't moved.

"Your mom should have dinner ready soon," he said, looking over at my bedroom door. "She's making a roast."

I nodded. He nodded, too. Then he turned and walked out of my room, but he didn't shut the door. I ran over once he was gone and shut it. Then I sat back down on my bed and stared at the door for a while.

## The Virgin Mary Tree

"They cure headaches," Joy told me. "But if you don't have a headache, they'll give you one."

The cookie she handed me looked a lot like an Oreo. It just had the word Hydrox stamped on it instead. I'd never heard of Hydrox, but it looked pretty normal. Hydrox sounded like something that might have been medicine, though.

I ate it and it didn't taste anything like medicine.

Nicky heaved a chunk of asphalt into the alley and it broke into a bunch of pieces. I worried for a minute that we would get in trouble for making a mess. The alley was all broken up already anyway, though. There were potholes all over the place and the road was pretty crumbly. It was just an alley between our block and the graveyard. Nobody really fixed it. You couldn't even see it from the graveyard because the graveyard was on a hill across from us. There were trees and rocks all over the hill and the graveyard fence was at the top so we could hang out there but the graveyard probably didn't care much about the shape it was in. The rock Nicky smashed didn't really make things that much worse.

"We should make a rope-swing," Joy told us. "This tree would be *perfect*."

She looked up at the tree. It did look like it would have been good for that. It was kind of gnarled and bent over the alley so it would have been easy to climb. We could have almost just walked up the trunk. It had a good strong limb, too. Right over the alley.

I still didn't think the cookie was medicine. Joy had probably made it up so we wouldn't have known her parents didn't buy her good cookies. If we couldn't have caught her on it then it was something to show off, not something to hide. I thought she made it up.

It was probably just a cheap cookie.

"We don't have a rope, though," I said. "Where are we going to get one?"

"My dad's got a rope," Nicky offered, rolling over a rock. "He'll let us use it. He was going to make me a rope swing with it anyway, so he won't mind."

We didn't pay attention. It wasn't true. Nicky was like that. There wasn't even a tree in Nicky's yard you could have put a rope swing on. They were all really tall. The limbs were all too high up. He was just lying again.

"We can use my jump rope." Joy beamed, holding it up.

"I don't know." I hesitated. "I don't think it'll hold us."

The jump rope was pretty ratty, like it had been left out in the rain too many times. It was white with rainbow bands and red plastic handles, but the rainbow bands were faded and the white was washed out. The rope was starting to fray, too. I saw little hairs sticking up all over it. I bet it worked fine as a jump rope, but wouldn't have for a rope swing.

"Sure it will. We'll tie it to that branch." Joy pointed. "You'll see."

She started climbing up the trunk of the tree. She wasn't dressed exactly right for climbing. She had on a skirt for one thing. It was an old-looking blue thing made out of some rough kind of stuff–like paper towel-rough. There were orange outlines of cowboys on it with lassos. It kind of looked like one of those poodle skirts in those old movies on Sundays on channel 42. I thought maybe I'd be able to see up it while she was in the tree. Her shoes gave her trouble, though. Some odd-looking saddle shoes. They didn't have good grip for climbing trees. She made it up, though.

"When I get to the branch, one of you needs to toss the jump rope to me," she yelled down to us.

"Okay," Nicky responded, not really paying attention. He was using the rope as a machete to cut down a patch of weeds.

Joy stopped to stand on one of the lower branches of the tree. She looked over at Chris's grandma's house. Chris's grandma lived by herself but sometimes Chris came to visit with his parents. He was fat. Other grandkids came sometimes, too. Joy just stared.

"Somebody was in the window!" She squealed.

"Probably Chris's grandma," I muttered. Nicky was still cutting down weeds with the jump rope.

I felt like I was starting to get a headache. Maybe she told the truth about the cookie after all.

"I think it was a *ghost*," Joy went on. "Maybe the ghost of Rennae Liddle. I read a book about her. She hung herself in her attic."

I looked up at the window. I didn't see anything. The window was dark. She probably hadn't seen anything either. Besides, that girl wouldn't have been in Chris's grandma's house. If she was in a book then she hadn't probably ever been to Omaha. I didn't remember ever having seen a book about any Omaha ghosts.

"I wouldn't hang myself in an attic," Joy said. "I'd do it right on the Virgin Mary tree in the cemetery. It's a maple right next to the big statue of Mary. It looks like she's pointing at it."

"You don't have an attic anyway," I said back. "Your room would be the attic if you had one. It's Jeanie's and Nadine's room, too. They'd probably see you."

Joy lived in a tiny house over on the next block. It was yellow. It was weird, too. There were only five rooms. Her parents' room was off the kitchen. Her dad had been in there one time I came over. He hadn't even had a shirt on. I thought he'd been sleeping, even though it was a weekday.

I didn't think Joy's dad liked me. I had thought maybe her mom liked me, but Joy had told me both of them said we couldn't go out after Joy told them she said she'd be my girlfriend. They'd never said anything to me, though.

"You know what we should do?" Joy quietly changed the subject as she climbed down the tree. "We should nail some boards to the trunk so we can climb up and down to the rope easier."

I decided not to point out that we didn't have any nails. Or boards. Or a hammer.

It didn't matter that we didn't have a rope so I guessed it wouldn't matter that we didn't have any of those other things either. It probably wasn't going to happen anyway.

"My dad has nails," Nicky chimed in, swinging the jump rope over to Joy. "He'll let us have some."

"*No* he *won't*, Nicky," I snapped. "Stop making things up! Your dad won't give us any nails. You always say he'll give us stuff, but he never does!"

"Yes he *will*."

"*No* he *won't*!" I shoved Nicky. He acted like he was going to shove me back, but then he didn't.

"Yeah, he will. Go ask him."

I wasn't going to ask him. If I had, he would have just said no. I wasn't his kid. He wasn't supposed to have to give me stuff. I would have been that kid begging for junk from other people's parents. Nicky knew that. I'd fallen for that before, but not that time.

"Hey," Nicky remarked. "Where's Joy?"

We looked around. She wasn't up or down the alley or down our block. She hadn't climbed the tree again, either. We looked up and saw Joy slipping quickly through one of our holes under the graveyard fence.

The fence was chain link and there were three strings of barbed wire at the top, less in some places where it'd broken off. Since we couldn't climb over, we usually dug holes under it so we could go inside. The graveyard people filled the holes in with cement eventually, but we just dug others.

Joy started running as soon as she was on the other side of the fence. She tore off into the graveyard. She had her jump rope wrapped around her neck.

"Where's she going?" Nicky scratched his head.

"I don't know..." I mumbled.

Something was wrong, though. She was running, but it wasn't for fun. People didn't have fun running with ropes wrapped around their necks. She was running fast, too, like she was trying to get away from something. But, no one was chasing her.

I couldn't figure out why she took off. Nicky and me hadn't said anything. I thought maybe it had something to do with the cookie. I thought maybe she had gotten mad that the rope swing wasn't going to work out. She would have gone home if she'd been mad, though. Instead she was running off into the graveyard toward the Virgin Mary statue she had been talking about.

Something was real wrong. I knew it. My stomach felt sick.

"*Don't just stand there!*" I screamed, running toward the fence.

Nicky ran off down the block. I ducked through the hole and took off after Joy. I had to find out what was wrong. I had to catch her.

We were really going to get in trouble if something happened and we hadn't helped. My parents would have yelled at me and asked me why I had just let her go. Her parents, too. They'd have said she was our friend and we were supposed to have helped. Or maybe they wouldn't have said it. They'd have thought it, though. They'd all have thought it when they looked at me. It wasn't fair. I didn't even know what was going on.

"Joy, *stop!*"

I grabbed her. She spun around, trying to get away. She was bawling. Her face was all twisted up and red. She kept pulling. I couldn't keep a hold of her hands. The rope seemed to be the only thing I was able to grab, but it started to choke her when I tried holding onto it. It was wrapped really tight around her neck, more like a noose than the lassos on her skirt. I thought maybe she hadn't been just talking.

"*Stop, Joy!* Where're you going? What's the matter?" I shouted at her, but she just kept pulling.

I didn't know what I was supposed to do. I knew I had to catch her, but I hadn't thought about what to do after I caught her. I couldn't figure out how they expected me to do anything. I was going to be in for it for sure if I didn't do something, but I couldn't think what kind of something I could do. She wouldn't stop to tell me what was the matter. I wasn't going to be able to do anything and they were all going to blame me.

I kind of gave up a little and stopped fighting as hard. I couldn't figure out how to stop her anyway. Joy broke away and ran off toward the far side of the graveyard. I didn't follow. There was nothing I could do. She wouldn't talk to me.

I thought I could tell them all I tried. I thought maybe that was going to be good enough. I walked back to the hole in the fence. I might have even gotten in trouble for having been in the graveyard. I wasn't supposed to go there at all. I still went a lot, but my parents didn't know that. They'd have yelled if they found out I went in. Or maybe worse.

I just didn't understand. She seemed fine. Not even mad. She had said that weird thing about hanging, but it wasn't really weird for her. Nothing else had happened. Nobody had said anything
mean. One second she was good and happy. Then she wasn't. I couldn't figure it out.

Joy's parents' car barreled by as I stood up after sliding through the hole under the fence. They were driving down the alley toward their little yellow house. Nicky must have run to tell and they went and got Joy. She was slouched over in the back seat. Her face was puffy and red. She didn't look at me as the car sped past, bouncing over all the potholes.

# But Nothing Was Better

"**S**ensitive," Mrs. Elden intoned. " S-e-n-s-i-t-i-v-e."
I marked that one down. Patrick Redding'd spelled it with an *a* instead of an *i*.

I was sitting at my desk. It had a metal base with the wood lid and the wood chair fixed together with pipe sorts of things. Everybody in my class was grading their neighbor's spelling test. Even with everybody there, the desks only took up a little bit of the middle of the room. My school was really old so the rooms were all big with tube lights hanging way up on the giant ceilings, and had huge old windows with wires inside the glass. Mrs. Elden sat up on the front of her square metal desk, and even with that the room was kind of empty.

"Upstanding." She went on. " U-p-s-t-a-n-d-i-n-g."

Mrs. Elden was my Core teacher. She had a mop of curly brown hair, triangle-shaped, and big round glasses with these funny bent-up wire rims. She looked like a mom.

That year they'd started rotating us some for classes. It was supposed to get us ready for junior high. Everybody had a Core teacher. You stayed with them for most subjects and whatever the rotating subject that they taught was. The other sixth graders went to Mrs. Elden for Spelling and Reading. My class went to Mr. Cartier for Social Studies and Ms. Rondo for Math.

The door at the front of my classroom cracked open.

We all looked up. Mrs. Elden looked up, too. It was the aide from the principal's office. She was an itty-bitty old woman, barely taller than most of us—if even that tall compared with some of the bigger kids. She never really talked—not to us, at least. She just smiled occasionally. She probably smiled because she liked kids.

Like now, for instance.

She smiled at Mrs. Elden. Mrs. Elden walked to the door. The aide handed her a note and Mrs. Elden read it.

Mrs. Elden looked at me. "Peter, Mrs. Galloway would like to see you in her office."

Peter was me. She handed me the note. The class was really quiet as I got up from my desk and left. I heard Mrs. Elden go on to the next spelling word as I shut the door. Maybe she was going to grade Patrick's test herself.

I wondered why Mrs. Galloway wanted to see me as I wandered down the hallway behind the aide. I looked at the note, but it was just a pass. It didn't say anything. The aide didn't say anything either. She just walked alongside me and was quiet.

I remembered I had gotten a hundred percent on a report about the Aztecs the week before. Maybe Mrs. Galloway was going to make me Student of the Month. I walked a little faster down the hall. She probably wouldn't have made me Student of the Month for that, but maybe.

The floors in the hall were wood. Some of the boards were darker than the others. I thought about sawing different colored bits of the boards apart. With a chainsaw. It almost made shapes. I could have had a life-sized jigsaw puzzle. I would need a chainsaw, though. That, and I'd need to get into the school when no one was there. I was pretty sure a chainsaw could cut into the floor easily. I'd never used one before, but they cut through pretty much anything.

It was busy around the main office. All the hallways in the school met in a big open area at the big staircase. The main office was there behind some glass walls. You had to walk through the door in the glass walls and then through a door in back to get to Mrs. Galloway's. There was a desk out in the open area in front of the glass walls for the student helper to sit at. I wondered why the student helper just hadn't brought the note. Usually the kid they picked ran stuff to classrooms, not the aide. I thought the aide just did office stuff or answered phones.

Mrs. Galloway was sitting down when I came in. She had a big old wood desk facing the door. It had to have been there as long as the school. I think she kept it to make her look important. She had a couple of couches too, one on each side of the door, like she wanted it to look like people just came in there and sat all the time. The couches were old, too. They were in pretty good shape, though, since nobody ever really did just come in and sit.

Mrs. Galloway sat up straight, hands folded. Her fingers pointed rigid like a long, thin pyramid. I stopped in the doorway. That's when I saw my friend, Joy, sitting on one of Mrs. Galloway's couches.

I started feeling sick. Joy was wearing the same rough blue cloth skirt with the orange outlines of cowboys twirling lassos she wore yesterday. The same saddle shoes. Her face was red and puffy again, all twisted, just like the day before. She looked kind of banged up. It looked like her face was wet, like she'd been crying.

She wasn't crying anymore, though.

"Peter," Mrs. Galloway said all formal, trying to act official. Her voice twanged a little. "Do you know why I called you down?"

"No," I lied. I said it too quietly. I wanted it to sound normal. Joy was on the couch. I had been too quiet, though. I looked drained like the time Joseph Bearn socked me in the stomach.

"I think you do know," Mrs. Galloway continued.

"No," I stuttered. I couldn't seem to get it. I wasn't convincing.

"Yesterday's…*incident* was very private, Peter."

Yesterday was at the cemetery. With the jump rope. Around Joy's neck. The running and the something sudden

going on and then Joy's parent's taking her home in their car
without saying anything.

It wasn't my fault.

"Peter, you shared something with other students that
was very personal for Joy," Mrs. Galloway continued. "Something she had not chosen to share."

Mrs. Galloway was acting all serious and proper, acting
like what she thought she was supposed to do. For some reason,
I couldn't stop thinking about when she gave everybody her
family's old peach cobbler recipe. Or what she did in a skit in the
talent show dressed like some old-time rich southern lady.

"To be entrusted with another person's privacy is very
special. Good people recognize how special such a thing is and
carefully protect it. Did you stop to think how making Joy's
personal matters public would make her feel?"

Mrs. Galloway waited, but I didn't say anything.

"I am very disappointed in you, Peter. I am
disappointed, and I believe Joy is disappointed as well."

My chest was pounding. My stomach cramped. I
couldn't breathe but I was breathing too hard at the same time.
They'd tell my parents and my dad would kill me. He'd never
listen to me if the school said I was bad. He'd be too mad.

"*No!* I only told Steven!" I screamed, desperate.

I had to make things better. I hadn't told Steven. I'd
told Mike and Patrick and Matt and everybody else I could tell.
Steven had just been there. It was my big news. I had seen
something big and I got to be the one to tell about it. I hadn't
thought I could ever get in trouble.

"Is this true?" Mrs. Galloway looked narrowly at me.
Joy didn't say anything.

I thought I might have almost been crying myself. "I only told Steven. He must have told everybody else."

Mrs. Galloway wouldn't have bought my story if I said I hadn't told anyone at all, but she'd believe Steven was the *really* bad one. He always got into trouble. He got held back in second grade. I mean, I was a little bad for telling Steven, but he was worse because he told *everybody*. It was a little okay that I told Steven. He was my best friend and everyone knows best friends tell each other things they're supposed to keep secret. *I was just acting guilty because I'd told him.* They'd believe that. It wasn't good, but it was better than things would have been otherwise.

"I think you should have a talk with Steven then. You should tell him how that was not the right thing for him to do and how disappointed you are in him," Mrs. Galloway concluded. She looked down at her desk and started writing on a piece of paper. "Steven's class would be in the gym right now."

I didn't move. I thought she was going to send the aide to fetch Steven.

Mrs. Galloway looked up at me. "I would like you to bring Steven here so you can speak with him in my office," she said.

She gave me the pass she'd been writing.

I got out of there quick. It was a nightmare, but I had kept everything from coming apart. I felt good when I got out of the office, until I remembered I was supposed to get Steven. Steven would deny it. He hadn't told anybody, after all. He'd never admit to it just to save me. He might even yell enough that they'd find out I lied.

I walked real slowly down to the gym.

The school didn't really have a gym. It was just a huge basement where we had P.E. and ate lunch. I had to go down some stairs. Then some more. Cement floors and cinder block walls that were painted a wet-looking gray.

I felt all that ground above crushing me as I made my way down.

We didn't have P.E. all the time. Maybe only once or twice a week. This sweaty black guy came in to teach it. Mr. Watt. It was usually a game of flag football or softball or something like that. One time we just played on these green plastic scooter things the school kept locked up in a big closet.

Steven's class wasn't doing anything when I got there. Just sitting in rows.

Mr. Watt saw me come in. "*Yeah?*" He said, chewing on something.

"Mrs. Galloway wants me to get Steven."

"You got a pass?" I showed it to him and he motioned to Steven. "Go and then come right back, hear? Don't just go running around the halls."

Steven nodded. He got up and walked towards me. I walked back up the steps out of the gym, hoping he'd follow me without asking anything.

"Why deoes Mrs. Galloway want to see me?" He asked as we walked down the hall.

"I don't know," I lied. "She just told me to go and get you."

"I got a new game," he said. "It's a racing one. You should come over after school so we can play it. I can only play until dinner, though. Scott's brother got a pitching machine and we're going to go over to his house later and practice."

I guess I didn't act too interested because he didn't say anything after that. He just walked behind me, right on into Mrs. Galloway's office. He froze when he saw Joy on the couch. He looked at Mrs. Galloway and then at me.

He looked like he knew something was up.

I had to be fast, catch him off guard. "You shouldn't have told people what I told you about Joy," I said to him. He jumped a little. Mrs. Galloway nodded. I tried to look as upset as I could. I had to act real and say what she'd told me to say. Then it'd be his word against mine. Steven looked confused. He looked how I should have made myself look. "Joy needed help and you made it worse," I went on.

"*What?*" Steven was starting to get angry as well as confused. He looked quick at Mrs. Galloway and then back at me. "I didn't tell, *you* did!"

I was shaking. I just had to do what I'd been told. Then this could all go away. All he had to do was let me yell at him. That would be enough. It would be the end of it. "No I didn't! You're lying!"

"*Boys*, stop!" Mrs. Galloway shouted, standing up and smacking her palms on the top of her desk

Her eyes looked wild. Both me and Steven looked at her. Joy just sat there on the couch not saying anything. Mrs. Galloway cleared her throat. She wiped her forehead with the tips of her long fingers and sat back down again. Her eyes were normal again. "Now then," she said quieter, "Steven, is it true that you told students about what happened the other day?"

"*No! He* was the one that—"

"Just answer the question," Mrs. Galloway interrupted, holding up her hand to stop him. She paused. "Now, Peter," she said, turning to me, "is it true, then, that you were the one who told and not Steven?"

"*No!*" I wailed.

She pursed her lips, waited before talking more. Her long fingers drummed lightly on the top of her desk. "Well," she turned to Joy, "it seems there just is no getting to the bottom of this. These boys are simply too ashamed to admit which one of them is really at fault here."

Joy started opening her mouth to say something.

"We certainly could bring in each student individually and find out the truth," Mrs. Galloway quickly said before Joy could talk, "but that would cause this ugly rumor to spread around even more. We don't want that, do we?"

Joy closed her mouth. She looked down at her shoes. The clock on Mrs. Galloway's wall hummed.

"No, that would not improve the situation at all. This unpleasantness needs to stop, not grow." Mrs. Galloway looked at us. "I am disappointed in both of you. I do not think either of you acted appropriately, regardless of who is actually responsible. Frankly, I do not think it is relevant. I am appalled the rumor was spread at all. I am sure you are both more involved than you maintain." She looked quick at Joy and then back at us.

Me and Steven just stood there, waiting.

"I want you both to think very long and hard about this. One or both of you acted inappropriately. I even suggest that you might inform the other students that you made it up, that it never happened. That would be the appropriate course of action. In any event, I do not want to hear of anyone mentioning this horrible business again, or anything similar. Am I understood?"

"Yes," both Steven and me replied quietly. Steven was looking down, frowning.

"Good, now I want you both to go right back to your respective classes."

We walked out at the same time, but Steven didn't say anything. He didn't even look at me. He just turned and walked off back toward the gym. I walked back to my class, but nothing was better.

# The Pipe

I blinked a couple times, lying on Steven's neighbor's grass with that Bobby kid from a couple blocks over. He hung out with us sometimes. Not that it did any good, blinking. The sun still burned, bright as it was. I closed my eyes, seeing little flashes in the dark. It was hot. Stuffy. Like I had a wool blanket over my face. I couldn't breathe so I opened my eyes again. I poked the dirt with a stick.

It was summer so we could do whatever we wanted, but I didn't want to do anything. We picked at melted tar in the street when the mailman showed up to deliver the mail. Then we walked around the block when Steven's neighbor started mowing his grass. Finally, we just sat on the lawn so we didn't have to pretend to do stuff next time someone came by, just to seem busy, so the kids on the block didn't think we couldn't find anything to do.

Nothing wouldn't have been so bad if everybody had been there. If Steven and all of us had done nothing together then it wouldn't have been lame. Doing nothing that day was lame, though, because me and Bobby were the only ones. Steven was at his uncle's farm. That dork, Nicky, and, Freddy, the jerk were each home inside, sick.

Even Joy wasn't home. She would have thought of something fun to do. Joy didn't hang out much anymore, though. She was always over at this other girl's house. She didn't even like her, she just liked the girl's brother. Even though he was weird and went around with zit cream on his face and ate glue off stamps.

Things were better when Joy still hung out.

The freshly mowed grass smelled great when we first sat down, kind of sweet.

By then it had started to smell gross, though. Kind of like garbage. Bobby didn't seem to care, but the grass had to have been scratchy. He didn't wear jeans like everybody else. Just those dopey short slacks. His shirt even had *buttons*, like that uniform from that Catholic school he went to. I bet it didn't keep out grass clippings. I didn't dress like that unless my parents made me go to church.

An ice cream truck turned onto the block and started to cruise by slowly, ringing the bell. We didn't get up, though, so he sped up again. I could have gone for some ice cream, but my pockets were empty, and Bobby never had any money, even though his parents had plenty. His parents had such nice stuff that they wouldn't even let us play in their house. They were probably afraid we'd break something.

Some days we'd try for freebies, but I didn't feel like it that day.

"We could go to the pond down by the steel mill, Peter," Bobby sighed, lazy. His neatly clipped brown hair was a little mussed from the grass. He quickly smoothed it and straightened it up again, even though it was still pretty combed. "Like throw rocks or just hang out or something."

"I guess," I replied, trying not to sound interested. "Could just hang out here, too."

"But," Bobby grinned, "*they* can see us. Nicky doesn't have anything to do but look outside. He'll snitch to Stevie."

Bobby always called Steven Stevie. Like he needed to prove stuff because he wore all those dorky clothes. And that girly, Scottish dancing thing his parents made him do, too. His face was even kind of girly, all thin and pointed like that Heather girl in my class last year. He never said it to Steven's face, though. Steven wouldn't have let him hang out with us anymore if he had. "You'll get razzed when he gets back."

I glared at him. It was true, but he hadn't needed to say it. He knew if I told Steven then Steven would have known I had done nothing, too. Bobby was just showing off. He was grinning, all stretched out on his back in the grass. One girly twig thin leg leaned over the other, kicking his dressy leather shoe. I had no real choice. "Whatever. It's as good a place as any to waste time."

"We could go for a swim," Bobby babbled as we walked.

He was just talking. The pond was all gross, full of all kinds of stuff. It was just some water in a ditch by the steel mill across the street from Joy's house.

The mill looked even more run down than the graveyard. I didn't know if they even made stuff there anymore. I guess they had to, though, because junk kept getting into the pond. The water swirled with rainbows and nasty pasty foam frothed all over the rocks.

It smelled like furniture polish. We didn't touch it. Ever.

We sat down by the pipe that ran over the ditch. The hill wasn't too steep so there were plenty of places to sit. There were lots of rocks, too, to throw down at the pond. Bobby grabbed one and chucked it. It clanged off of the pipe and fell all the way down with a *splush*.

The pipe was thick enough for somebody to crawl through. It came out from the other side at the steel mill and went into the hill across from Joy's house. It was pretty long and high up from the pond below. It just sat there, though. I didn't know what the dumb thing was supposed to be for.

Bobby stared at the pipe. We focused on the pipe a lot. One of us was always talking about running across it to the steel mill. None of us ever did, though. Steven almost did one time. Got up there and everything, but then he just froze. We hadn't said anything. Not even Bobby. Nobody expected anybody to do it.

"I think if I just got a good head start, I could run right across," Bobby said. His voice made him sound far away.

I didn't listen. He was starting up again. Normally, I would have done it, too, but I didn't want to right then. It just seemed dumb. I'd have rather sat in the dirt—just like I was doing—wondering what Joy was doing right then over at that other girl's house.

"Yep," he went on when I didn't say anything. "Fast enough and I couldn't fall."

"Mmm," I said, hoping he'd realize I didn't care and stop talking. He didn't, though. He got it, but he got pissed instead.

"*What?* Don't you think I can do it? I can."

I sighed and threw a rock. "Don't be like that, Bobby."

Bobby crossed his arms and tried to flex. It didn't work. His arms were sticks just like his legs. "You don't think I'm for real. I am."

"I don't care. I don't feel like doing all that today." Joy was probably messing around with that girl's brother right then. Like that time she dumped that whole bottle of perfume on his head.

Bobby still looked mad. His thin face was wrinkled in a frown. "All *what?*"

I sucked on my lip. "You know, pipe stuff."

"I'm not just talking." Bobby sneered, trying to do it all cool like Steven did. "You think I'm am, but you can't know."

"Come off it. We all talk, but that's it. I'm not even saying anything bad about you. I just don't want to be dumb today and I don't want to listen to you do it either."

"Hey! Say what you want about Steven and you guys," Bobby yelled. "That's not me. I got nads."

"Calm down." He was really mad, face all red, like the fire hydrant that used to be outside his house before his parents got the city to move it. "I'm not saying you don't have nads."

"I'll do it," he said, calm but sounding far away again. "I won't chicken out like Stevie."

"I know, Bobby. Let's just talk about something else. That's all I mean."

Bobby didn't say anything. I got curious and looked over. He was staring at the pipe. "Hey, I got an idea," I said, trying to distract him. "Let's go play basketball. Steven won't be there to hog the ball today. We can use his hoop. His mom won't mind if we don't hang off it like that one time Joy dared us to."

"I bet you really think I'm like that, just talking."

"Huh? *Bobby! Come on*, stop screwing around with that crap already!"

"I'm not screwing around with anything."

"Look, Bobby, why even do that? It's stupid. You'd probably get hurt. We're not that dumb so we just talk. It's retarded, but *so what?*"

"But I don't pretend. If I say something, I'll do it. You guys are losers if you lie like that."

"It's just something *to do*."

"It's *fake*. I'm not a faker."

I threw up my hands. "So don't talk. Whatever. That's fine with me."

"*No*," he said slowly. "You'll still think I won't. And you can't think that if I actually do it."

"*Bobby*!" I sat up quick. "Don't be stupid. Seriously. You'll fall and break a leg or something."

"*So?* Are you saying I'm scared now?"

"*No*! It's just dumb. It's a stupid pipe. You don't have to show me anything."

Bobby stood up, puffing out his skinny bird chest. "You just don't want me to so you can keep thinking I wasn't going to. Then you can laugh at me and not feel like a chicken."

"That's not it. I *really* believe you will, honest. Just don't, okay?"

"You can talk all you want. I'm doing it."

"I can't let you, Bobby," I said, standing up, but Bobby was already on the end of the pipe. He had jumped on there when he saw me.

"You can't stop me. You're not my dad."

"Bobby, *don't*!" I sounded like I was whining. I hated that. "I'll get in trouble," I said, but I didn't know how to stop him. It was just like when Joy ran off crying with the rope around her neck again. I couldn't do anything.

"I'll run if you try. You'd be too late. Not that you would anyway, you don't have any nads. Just like Stevie."

"Course I'm scared. You should be, too." I had to stop him, but I couldn't make myself get up there. I kept telling myself he'd just run anyway if I had. It wouldn't have helped.

"I'm not scared. I'll show you."

"*Bobby! Don't!*"

Bobby set himself to run, tongue sticking out a little from the side of his thin pursed lips, and smoothed his hair with one hand. He looked down the pipe and then over at the steel mill. Then he took a deep breath and went for it—not walking or inching, but *running*. Full speed, down the pipe, looking straight ahead.

Then, one of his feet slipped.

Nothing tripped him. His foot just slid out funny. Maybe his dressy leather shoes were too slick. Not like sneakers. He tried to catch himself and I lurched forward to grab him, but my feet didn't go.

Bobby fell. I saw him. He landed with a loud *crunch* on the rocks in the pond. His eyes were closed and he didn't move. He looked like he was dead.

# Cards

"**G**et out of the way, Terence!" I yelled as I pulled on the chains and swung forward. I was over at the park across the street from my new house in Oregon with a bunch of the kids from the neighborhood. "I'm going to jump."

Danny looked up a little. He sat on a swing like a big old slug. Not swinging really, just swaying around a little scuffing the dirt with his shoes. The dirt got his black sweat pants all dusty. He probably didn't care. He always had those dingy things on.

"Yeah, Terence, you big baby," Benji sneered, dangling from the overhead bar above the swings and kicking his feet. "You're always in the way. Why don't you go home? Nobody even likes you."

Terence waddled off to the side, looking to see if he was far enough away. He pulled up his sagging shorts as he went, one-handed because he clutched a loose deck of cards in the other. His shirt was too big for him, too—loose from being all worn out. It had a cartoon of a guy fishing. It was probably from Goodwill.

"But I'm moving today," he whined after he got out of the way. "I'm not going to be able to play with you guys anymore."

I shot backwards, leaning forward and pulling on the thick metal chains. They were all dull from being outside in the rain and even looked a little rusty. I hit the top of my swing and gripped the chains, feeling like I was falling for a second. Then I leaned back and swung forward again. As I swung out, I pushed off from the chains, sticking my feet out, and flew through the air. I landed hard, but ran forward through the park until I slowed down.

"Good jump," Benji said as I turned around to walk back. He hung from the overhead bar above the middle swing. "I got further last time though."

"No you didn't," Danny said. "*Liar.*"

"I know you are, but what am I?"

Danny poked around in the dirt under his swing with the toe of his shoe some more. I just looked over at how my swing was still moving just a little bit. Benji still thought Pee-wee was cool. He even got his mom to let him get his hair cut like that. That show was dumb, though. It was for little kids. Benji was littler than me and Danny, but not real little like Terence. Benji still liked some stuff like that.

I walked back to the swings. They were a lot bigger than the ones on the old set I used to have before we moved after Bobby got hurt. It had all these thick steel pipes, worn dull like the chains. There were three swings all in a row and a slide sticking off the side, going the same direction as the swings.

Terence was off over by the slide, still holding onto the cards. "Anybody want to play? I got cards." He held them up like they were a quarter he'd just found. "We could play."

Benji and Danny ignored him. Benji was busy trying to pull himself up on the overhead bar. Danny was still just sitting there, but that's all he ever did. If he had to move much for a game, he didn't play. He barely even left his house. I was surprised he was outside right then. Whenever I came over he looked like he'd been napping.

Terence was the first kid I'd met after we moved. He just came up and asked if I wanted to play. I'd just been sitting outside by myself.

He was pretty little, though, so I made him show me where the other kids in the neighborhood lived. He took me to Danny first because he lived right next door, but Danny didn't like to do very much.

Benji always had something to do, but we weren't supposed to hang out after we broke his bathroom window with the ladder trying to peep in on his sister in the shower. We had to hang out at the park where my parents couldn't see us because of the park fence.

I sat back down on the swing. "Cards are too much work. We're just hanging out," I said and started to swing again. Not hard like I was going to jump this time, just easy.

"They're probably stolen anyway," Benji muttered. "Your mom doesn't have any money to buy you stuff. I saw the police over at your house last week. Maybe they were there because she stole you those cards."

"No they're *not!*" Terence tugged at the bottom of his Goodwill shirt. It was already too big. He wouldn't be able to wear it if he stretched it out much more.

"Then why were the police there?"

Terence picked at a band-aid on his forehead with his free hand. It looked all stained and dirty. "I don't know. I was in bed. I'm supposed to stay in bed when my mom puts me there."

I'd seen it out my window, too. I saw all these blue and red lights on my bedroom walls and looked out. There were three police cars. One of them was even pulled up on the lawn. Terence's mom was leaning out the upstairs window and wouldn't unlock her door. At least, I think it was her. I'd never seen Terence's mom outside. She was white, too, and Terence was sort of black.

I asked my dad later what was going on over there, but he told me I should mind my own business.

"If the cards were stolen, the police would have taken them," Danny said. His sweat pants were sagging down and he struggled to pull them up. They didn't really fit him. Maybe he liked them that way so he could get fatter and not need new ones. It looked like he was still wearing his pajamas.

"Maybe they didn't find them," Benji countered. He didn't sound like he really believed it, though.

It was stupid. The police didn't come to people's houses for a pack of cards. The cards looked like they probably came free with something anyway.

Benji was still trying to get up on the overhead bar. He kicked a foot up over the bar and tried to scramble up. He just kind of hung there, though, when he got tired. He wasn't strong enough to get up there. It was just a bar. There was nowhere for him to sit even if he did get all the way up.

"We could play *crazy eights*," Terence offered. "I learned that game."

I grabbed the chains and pulled, standing with my feet on my swing. The thick blue rubber seat bent around my foot, trapping it in there. I kicked and pulled at the chains so I swung, standing, back and forth.

"So, what do you guys want to do, Peter?" Benji asked.

"I don't know." I kicked harder.

Terence looked at us.

"There's nothing to do," Danny mumbled. He brushed a little of the dust off his sweat pants. Not enough to help how they looked, though.

Benji gave up trying to climb and dropped to the ground. "I got a new basketball. We could go play over on the court."

Terence shifted from one foot to another and chewed on his lip. I saw the cards still clutched tightly in his hand.

"It's too hot," Danny complained.

"We could at least play *HORSE*. Then we wouldn't have to run around as much."

"I guess."

"Except for you, Terence," Benji told him. "You can't play because you're too short to make any baskets. You always want do-overs."

Terence looked like he was going to cry. His eyes were all watery and snot was dripping a little from his nose. He wiped at it with his hand and sniffed. Then he wiped the same hand on his Goodwill shirt.

"Doesn't *anybody* want to play cards with me?"

Benji looked over at the basketball court. Danny just looked at his feet. Neither of them said anything. I looked at them and then at Terence.

"Nobody?"

I couldn't stop thinking. Nobody wanted Terence around. It sucked always having him following us, but it must have been worse to actually *be* him. This was all he was getting for his last day in the neighborhood.

"I'll play a couple of games," I said, adding, "but just a couple."

"Okay," Terence beamed. "We can play on the slide."

He waddled over and plopped down next to the slide. Then he started trying to shuffle. He couldn't really shuffle, so he just kept stacking parts of the deck in different orders. It didn't matter. I didn't care if I won or not.

The metal slide was hot from being in the sun. The cards stuck to it a little. I had to hold my arms above the slide instead of resting my elbows or else I'd burn myself. Benji and Danny looked at me.

"Can we play *crazy eights?*"

"Sure," I said. I didn't care. Besides, he probably didn't know any other games.

Terence bounced up and down while he passed out the cards. "I'm going to deal, but I want to go first, okay?"

"Sure, whatever."

It wasn't that bad. Only a couple of games. That wouldn't take too long. I didn't really want to, but I could do it. I didn't really feel like playing *HORSE* anyway.

# Biography

*Photograph by Shannon Kaye Mooney*

David S. Atkinson's writing has appeared in *[PANK]*, *The Rumpus, Grey Sparrow Journal, Interrobang?!*, *Atticus Review*, *JMWW, The Writing Disorder* and others. *Bones Buried in the Dirt* is *his first book. His url* is http://davidsatkinsonwriting.com/ He spends his non-literary time working as a patent attorney in Denver. He does not care for mushrooms.

# Acknowledgements

There are a number of authors whom I should thank first of all for the debt I owe to their work. *The House on Mango Street* by Sandra Cisneros both helped me understand what I wanted to do with this book and showed me how a master would do it. Someday, I hope to have a chance to thank her. Similarly, Lewis Nordan's *Music of the Swamp* taught me more about writing through a child than I will ever truly realize. Sadly, the passing of Lewis in the last year means I will never have a chance to thank him.

I also want to thank everyone involved in the University of Nebraska MFA program. This includes Jenna Lucas Finn, Richard Duggin, and Art Homer for all that they did to make the program live. This also includes each of my mentors: Lee Ann Roripaugh, Amy Hassinger, Charles Wyatt, and Brent Spencer. However, this book owes a much bigger debt than just that. In fact, I would be hard pressed to find someone in the program that I did not owe thanks to for something good in this collection.

Thanks as well to all the journals that gave homes to various pieces of this collection: *Grey Sparrow Journal*; *The Writing Disorder*; *The Lincoln Underground*; *C4: The Chamber Four Lit Mag*; *Split Quarterly*; *Cannoli Pie*; *Children, Churches and Daddies*, and *Fine Lines*. I owe them big, just as I owe Diane Smith (who gave this collection a chance), Joseph Michael Owens (who labored through my first round of edits) and *Karen Gettert Shoemaker (who delighted me by agreeing to write a forward for this book)*.

Last, it's weird, but I want to thank the person who had a few loud words with me over a particularly bad story I had written. I wrote the original incarnation of "The Pipe" as an answer...and that started everything.

# Contributors

**Joseph Michael Owens**, Editor, is the author of the "collectionovella" *Shenanigans!* (Grey Sparrow Press, 2012) and has written for *[PANK] Magazine*, *The Rumpus*, *The Houston Literary Review*, and *Specter Literary Magazine*. He is the current blog editor for *InDigest Magazine* and the web content editor for *The Lit Pub*. Additionally, he manages *Category Thirteen*, a website that focuses primarily to the hectic (and sometimes haptic) process of writing. Joe lives in Omaha with four dogs and one wife.

**Timm Burgess** is an Animation Director and Compositor. He noted, "Photography has always played an important part in my work, and all the skills as a compositor and rostrum cameraman have benefited my approach to photography. I love mixing media and textures and making the image how I see it. HDR photography is a big part of my work today and my work has been exhibited in galleries here in the UK."

**Karen Gettert Shoemaker** is the author of *Night Sounds and Other Stories* (Dufour Editions, 2002; UK edition - Parthian Press, 2006) and the forthcoming novel *The Meaning of Names* (Red Hen Press, 2014). She has published stories in the *Prairie Schooner*, the *London Independent*, *The South Dakota Review*, *Fugue*, *Kalliope*, and others. Her stories and poems have been anthologized in *A Different Plain: Contemporary Nebraska Fiction Writers; Times of Sorrow/Times of Grace; An Untidy Season;* and *Nebraska Presence: An Anthology of Poetry*. She has received fellowships to Brush Creek Ranch Artist Colony and the Kimmel Harding Nelson Center. She is the recipient of a Nebraska Center for the Book Award for Fiction; two Independent Artist Fellowships from the Nebraska Arts Council, and a Nebraska Press Award for Feature Writing. She is a faculty mentor with the University of Nebraska MFA in Writing Program.

**Diane Smith**, Publishing Editor, BA, MSE was born in the United States. She often writes about those with little power or visibility in society. Publishing has become her second career.

# Reprint Permissions

"The Pipe," was first published in an earlier form in *Fine Lines*, Summer 2007

"The Virgin Mary Tree," was first published in *Grey Sparrow Journal*, May 20, 2011

"Boys Chase Girls," was first published in *SPLIT Quarterly*, issue 3, June 30, 2011

"But Nothing was Better," was first published in *Cannoli Pie*, July 2011 (reprint permission for this story could not be obtained as the journal is no longer in operation)

"Stranger," was first published in *C4: The Chamber Four Lit Mag*, issue 2, Fall 2011

"Training Part 1" and "Training Part 2" were first published combined in *Children, Churches and Daddies Magazine,* v. 228, January, 2012

"Burden of a Little Brother," was first published in *The Lincoln Underground,* Summer 2012

"The War" was first published in *The Writing Disorder*, Winter 2012

Made in the USA
Charleston, SC
22 February 2013